140 Degrees

NASH NELSON

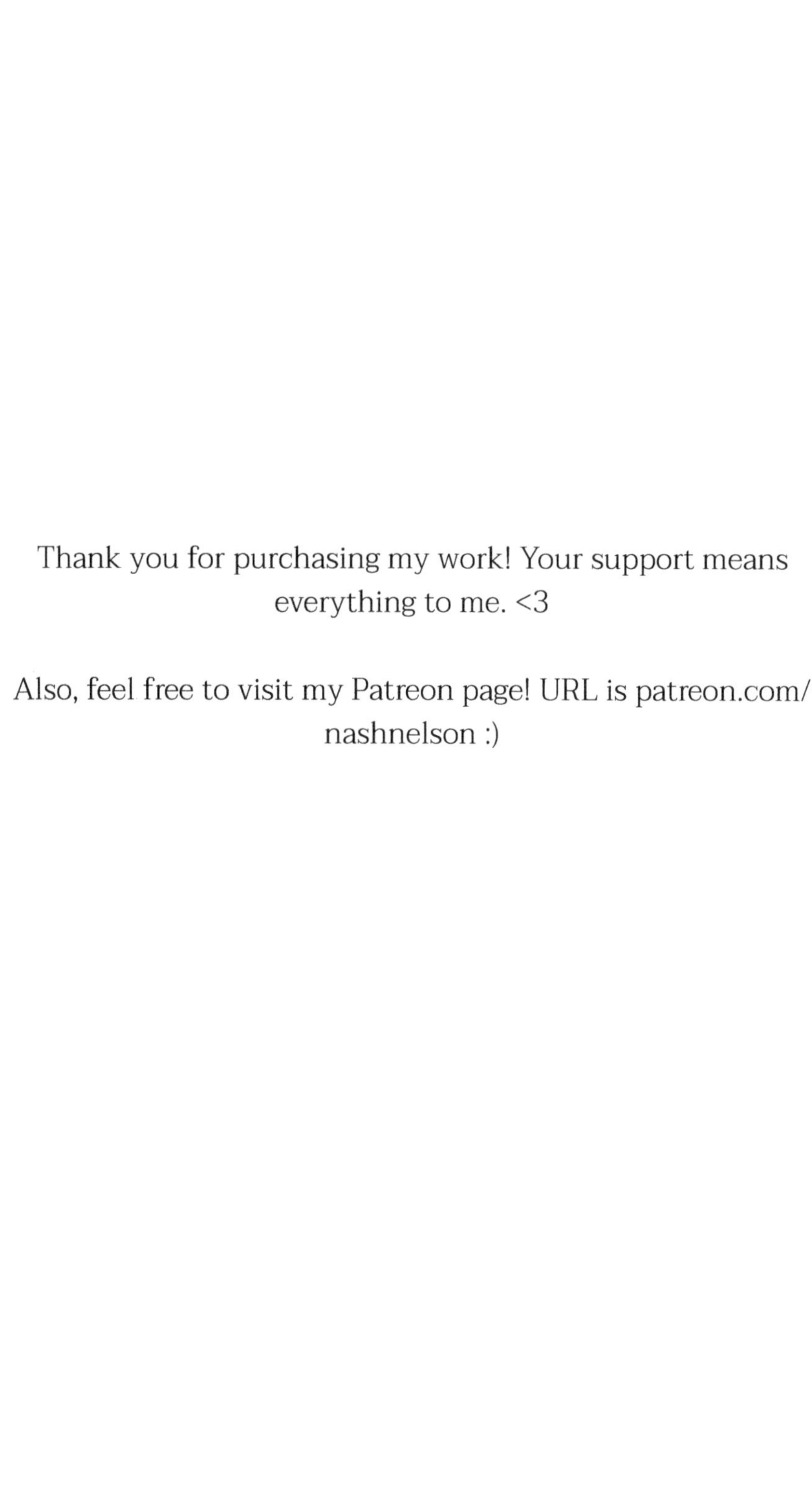
Thank you for purchasing my work! Your support means everything to me. <3

Also, feel free to visit my Patreon page! URL is patreon.com/nashnelson :)

Contents

140 DEGREES

Chapter One

The Road To Las Vegas

"You guys ready to fucking party?"

Barry scowled at his friend Chelsea as he wiped the sweat off his forehead. He was currently driving through the hottest place in the entire United States of America: Death Valley. The temperature read a shocking 109 degrees on the dashboard of his Chevy Malibu. He'd always heard that the desert was hell to drive through, but he never thought he'd experience it for himself.

And he had his love-struck best friend and two angry women to contend with, on top of all that.

Life just wasn't fair.

"Chels, knock it off. I said I was sorry for not having the money to afford a plane ticket."

The brunette with blonde streaks snorted and took a puff on her cigarette. "All you had to do was ask your mom for money."

"Yes," Barry argued. "Because she can just simply materialize money out of thin air, just to give to her only son for a trip to Vegas."

Chelsea glared at him, her green eyes glimmering under the bright desert sun. "If she can't do that, what good is she?"

Frustration rotted into his brain, but he refused to acknowledge her callous comment. She was trying to get him angry; it's what she did best. Why did he even agree to let her tag along with his friends? She was dating his best friend, sure. Sasha thought the world of her, true. But surely, he had to notice that she was a colossal bitch.

Barry sighed.

Love makes men do stupid things.

"Cool it, babe," said the brunette stallion himself. Sasha pulled Chelsea in and planted a kiss on her cheek. "Barry is driving us. The least you can do is show a little appreciation for him."

Barry smirked up at the rear-view mirror. "Thanks, man."

Alas, the blonde college student couldn't exactly complain about his best friend thinking with his dick. For the fourth passenger aboard this crazy train was Rikki Simmons. Redheaded and quiet, she stared outside the window as they drove through the desert. Her and Barry had a few conversations before, but she was really good friends with Chelsea.

Sasha did a little sweet talking and boom.

Rikki agreed to join the trio; much to Barry's benefit.

The young man found himself enthralled by Rikki. She wasn't like Chelsea, who was a haughty bitch who never shut up. The red head spoke very little and seemed to be rather pleasant. Whenever she did speak, she said something profound and intelligent.

Barry remembered the first time he heard her speak. They'd been in the same English course all semester, and he never once heard her talk. He was convinced she was mute!

But then she read a paper to the class, giving a literary analysis on *Fight Club*. Like a beautiful hymn, she discussed facets about the story Barry had never considered before, such as the homosexual undertones and symbolism behind the fight club itself. Her gentle tone, the words coming out of her mouth; it was magical. And the fact that she wasn't wasting her breath on some boring drivel like *Gone With the Wind* made him even happier!

Barry knew it was love right then and there.

Even if she was frustrated by the desert heat.

Rikki turned to face Barry, meeting his gaze through the rear-view mirror. "Can you turn up the A/C, please?"

Not wasting another moment, Barry turned the knob for the air conditioning, sending gale into the faces of everyone in the vehicle. He, himself, sighed with sweet relief as the sweltering hot was cast away. It allowed him to pretend he wasn't in the desert.

"Thank you, Barry."

The blonde grinned like an idiot. She remembered his name! He made enough of an impression that she felt him worthy of knowing. She still didn't know him, of course. But perhaps she was eager to!

"You're welcome, Rikki."

The red head smiled back. Barry's heart puttered like an awakening car engine. She was enjoying his company. He knew he needed to start a conversation with her, but he hadn't the first idea of what tool would be best suited for breaking the ice between them.

What did he talk about?

The weather?

The time?

Horses?

Was she even a horse girl?

Strategically, Barry knew he couldn't just solicit her for sex. She very likely wasn't that kind of girl, which made the blonde like her even more. Any girl that quiet was bound to be a virgin, blossoming with age and developing a libido that could only be sated by gentlemen oh so attracted to them. And Barry was a gentleman.

"So," the blonde started, manning up and making the first move. "Where are you from?"

Rikki looked out her window. "Pennsylvania."

Barry nodded in acknowledgement. "Must be very cold up there, compared to here."

The red head sighed. "You can say that again. I used to hate the cold; I've grown to miss it dearly. California just isn't cold enough."

He shrugged. "If you go north up to Eureka, it's pretty chilly. I'd know; I'm from there."

"Really?" Rikki asked with a smile. "Any must-sees I should know about in Eureka?"

She was engaging him in the conversation!

Jackpot!

"Well," he said, turning around to face the pretty girl. "There's always the Sequoia Park Zoo. That gets lots of tourists. You like pandas?"

The girl chuckled. "Sure."

"You'll love them at the zoo, then. There's also this awesome ramen shop just next door to my--"

Suddenly, Chelsea started screaming. "Look at the fucking road, Barry!"

He turned back around just in time to feel something slamming into the front end of his Chevy Malibu. Barry was forced forward into his steering wheel. Like clockwork, the airbag deployed. "*Ack!*"

After the longest five seconds of his life, Barry shoved the airbag out of his face. "Oh *fuck*, is that blood?" Due to the force of the collision, the airbag had hit him hard enough to bloody his nose on it. "Great, just my luck."

"*That's* what you're upset about?!" Chelsea growled. "You just wrecked your car, and your *nose* is what troubles you? Do you even care about the dog?"

Barry squinted up at the rearview mirror. "We hit a dog big enough to deploy the airbag?"

Sasha gave his girlfriend a quizzical look. "Dog? There was a dog out here?"

"Yes!" Chelsea shrieked. "Go out and look yourself! He's probably dead, poor thing."

Not even rolling his eyes at her hysterics, Barry unclipped his seatbelt and exited his car. He whipped around to see the damage on his car. Much to his horror, the front end was crushed and his engine was smoking. What left him confused was what he had hit.

There was no dog.

Not a large rock.

Not a human being.

Nothing at all.

Chapter Two

The First Hour

"What do you mean there's nothing there?!" Chelsea crowed from the back seat.

Rikki opened her door and rushed over to join Barry. She looked at the damaged front end, mouth agape. "There's...there's nothing here?"

The sounds of Sasha and Chelsea unclipping their seatbelts clicked faintly as the couple also rushed outside the vehicle. Sure enough, they also saw nothing. "I don't get it," Chelsea remarked. "I saw a dog. We hit a very big dog!"

"How big are we talking?" Sasha inquired.

With her left hand, the brunette with the blonde streaks held her hand up to Sasha's belly button. Given that his best friend was nearly seven feet tall, Barry shook his head. "Impossible, something that big wouldn't just disappear without us noticing."

"I'm telling you, I saw it," Chelsea argued. "Besides, how else can you explain the sudden crash? What caused it, if not a huge dog?"

Sasha nodded. "She's got a point, man. Even if we don't see it right now, something caused this to happen."

With a loud growl, Barry kicked the front end of his car. "I'm gonna find what did this and fuck it up," he ran a hand through his mid-length hair and turned away from his crew. "My parents are gonna kill me. Dad just made the final payment on this thing."

"What about us?" Chelsea asked frantically. "We're stranded out here in the fucking desert!"

Sasha rubbed her left shoulder. "It's okay. We have plenty of water in the trunk, remember? Packed just for the drive through Death Valley."

The woman batted his hand away. "Oh fantastic! We got water, but no wheels!"

Barry growled, stepping back over to the driver's side door. "Maybe we can fix it."

"Since when have you been a mechanic, Barry?" Sasha asked, tilting his head.

The blonde didn't look at him as he pulled the lever to pop his hood. "Never. Now's as good a time as any to learn." Barry stepped back in front of the car and opened the hood. Instantly, he was kissed on the lips by a flowing torrent of smoke. Coughing, the young man waved the fumes away from his face.

"Ack! What the fuck?" Barry didn't know much about cars, but even he knew a smoking engine was always a bad sign.

"There's no point in trying to fix it," Rikki commented, making Barry take his attention off the engine. "It's smoking and your airbag deployed. This car is totaled."

"That's just fucking great," Chelsea moaned. "Now what are we going to do?"

Barry looked up at the sky, away from the hot sun. He closed his eyes, saying a small prayer. "God, get me through this," he opened his eyes and looked back at his crew. "Does anyone here have a signal on their phone?"

At that point, everyone pulled their cell phones from out of their pockets. "Nothing," Sasha reported.

"Me neither," Chelsea said.

Rikki just shook her head.

Growing desperate, Barry held his phone up, trying to get some service. Much to his luck, he had one full bar. "I got one!" He quickly clicked his mother's speed dial entry, also putting the call on speaker.

First ring, and Barry's heart was threatening to fire up into his throat.

Second ring, and Chelsea was biting her nails.

Third ring and despair begin to sink in.

"This is Kathleen Waters. I am unavailable at the moment. Please leave your name and number and I'll get back with you shortly. Okay bye!"

Barry rose his voice as the beep sounded. "Hey Mom, it's Barry. Listen, I need you to call me as soon as possible. It's an emergency. Love you. Bye," he ended the call and sighed deeply. "Fuck!"

Rikki cleared her throat. "If I may make a suggestion?"

"Shoot," Sasha answered.

The red head looked at Barry, frown as big as a crescent moon. He hated seeing her like that. They didn't know each other very well, but she was still too beautiful to be upset. "We have lots of water, right? And I brought some sunscreen in my bag. We can stay out here for a little while. Staying in the car will just make the heat even worse."

"But it's so fucking hot out here," Chelsea whined. "I've only been outside the car for a few minutes, and I'm already covered in sweat."

Barry rolled his eyes.

She wasn't covered in that much sweat.

"The heat builds up in enclosed spaces. If we need to sit down, we can get inside the car as long as the windows are down."

The streaked brunette scoffed. "So, we're stuck in the blistering heat?!"

"Do you have a better idea?" Barry antagonized. "Because we don't have many other options."

A light bulb went off in Sasha's head. "Why not call your insurance and see if they can get a tow truck to save us?"

The blonde snapped his fingers. "Smart man! I can't believe I didn't think of that." Barry rushed over to the passenger side of the car, which nobody had sat in because Barry didn't like people touching him; it was a long story. He couldn't stand being touched, even if it's just a graze. If anyone was going to touch him, it would be under his terms and more intimate. Sitting beside someone in a car wasn't intimate.

Barry opened the door and began searching through his glove compartment. He pulled his printed insurance card and dialed the number for insurance into his phone. Holding the device up to his ear, he listened to the rings.

He was greeted by a machine.

He was prompted to press through buttons.

One for English, one for roadside assistance, three for towing services.

"You're the fourth person in the queue. Your call is very important to us."

Barry gritted his teeth. Why did people have to be ahead of him? He had an emergency!

Five minutes passed. "*You're the fourth person in the queue. Your call is very important to us.*" Five more minutes passed, and the message repeated. Barry threw his arm up.

"Mother*fucker*! How long does it take to call a tow truck?"

Five more minutes dragged on by. "*You're the fourth person in the queue. Your call--*"

Barry angrily hung up, which didn't win the favor of Chelsea. Then again, what did besides Sasha? "Why the hell did you hang up? We need a tow truck!"

"Because you can only wait so long in a virtual queue," Barry growled.

"Try it again, man," Sasha said. "We can't sit out here all day."

The blonde looked at his phone and bit his bottom lip. "I'll wait ten more minutes and call back."

Rikki, who had been quiet for some time, nodded her head. "See to it that you do."

Chapter Three

A Cold Shoulder

It was the year 2012. Barry was only seven years old, visiting Los Angeles for his father's thirty-sixth birthday. His old man wanted to see his favorite band from back in the day, Metallica. "I've never been to a show before," he'd explained. "I'd like to do it just once before I'm forty, you know?"

The young boy didn't care; he just enjoyed the drive. Unlike most children his age, he didn't mind travelling. If anything, he longed for it. The world was a big place! Why stay in Eureka when there's so much more of California to explore?

He couldn't deny that he also longed for the food. His mother had mentioned a super good seafood place with the biggest crab that anyone had ever seen. Barry loved crab; it was fun to clip the shell off and devour the savory meat. "Dad," the boy said. "Can we go to Hollywood, too? I wanna see if I can find any celebrities!"

His dad chuckled. "At least you're only wanting to do that. I think I'd die if you decided to become a child star. Too much paparazzi!"

"Not to mention the drugs and mental illness," his mom commented. "So many child stars end up screwy in the head when they grow up."

Barry leaned forward in the back seat of his dad's Honda HR-V. "Why do they do that?"

"Probably stress, Son," his old man remarked. "All the cameras, lack of privacy, and strict deadlines can drive anyone insane, let alone a kiddo such as yourself."

The kid blew a raspberry. "Phooey! I wouldn't go crazy. I'd be too busy being big and strong! I wanna be a commando and shoot at bad guys trying to overthrow the government!" Barry held his hands up and made finger guns. "Brrr! Pew pew pew! I'll get you, you son of a gun! Brrr!"

His parents looked at each other, grinning. "He's definitely your son, Greg. All those action movies you watch."

His dad rolled his eyes. "He'll outgrow it by the time he's a moody teenager. Then it will be gorefest horror movies for days!"

"Ugh," his mom groaned. "Don't even joke like that. You know how much I hate blood."

"But it's so cool, Mom!" Barry argued. "Like when it gushes out of bad guys like a super soaker. Psssssssh!"

The woman grimaced. "Make that sound one more time and you're eating vegetables all week."

The happy family all broke out into laughter as they drove south on the highway to the city of angels. The weather was nice the entire drive, nice and sunny with cumulus clouds resembling scoops of ice cream floating in the sky. Young Barry couldn't have been any happier if he tried, and once the family arrived in Los Angeles, the child stared at the sights. Mouth agape, he looked all around the outside of his window on the driver's side of the car.

"Woah! Look at all the lights! And the row of palm trees! Cool!" The evening sky shimmered with stars and an pomegranate sunset. It was no aurora borealis, but it was easily the second prettiest sky Barry had ever seen up until that point in time. "Is this what it's like in Las Vegas, Dad?!"

His father rolled his eyes playfully. "I told you before, Son. I'm not from Vegas; I'm from Boulder City. But no, Las Vegas is much more blinding at night."

The boy uttered another wow before finally blinking for the first time since arriving. The lights hurt his eyes, but he didn't care. Eureka didn't quite hold a candle to this place. The city of angels was a novelty that would surely generate memories that he'd cherish for years to come.

Even the hotel was beautiful. Once his father paid for parking, the family grabbed their bags and headed inside. Upon entry, Barry was stunned by the size of the lobby. It looked like something straight out of a millionaire's mansion. There was marble flooring, a large fountain front and center, a lounge and cafeteria combination, and the ceiling seemed to be miles away from the ground. He wouldn't have been surprised if there was a swimming pool somewhere in the massive hotel!

His mother and father walked up to the front desk to check into the room. Meanwhile, the child ran around the lobby. He loved car trips, but he also needed to stretch his legs after the twelve-hour drive from Eureka. And what better way to stretch than to run like a roadrunner?

As he ran around the lobby, Barry caught quick glances at the nearby guests. He was the only child in the room, and he was surrounded by equal parts smiles and scowls. Adults were funny, he thought to himself. They could be the coolest people in the world, but they could also be old fuddy-duddies who sucked the fun out of everything like vampires.

That didn't bifront him, so long as he could enjoy his vacation.

And so, the child ran around and around in circles. "Barry, stop that!" his mother ordered from the front desk. "You're going to make yourself sick!"

Doing as he was told, the child stopped in his tracks and breathed heavily. "This place is so cool," he murmured to himself. The neighboring adults eventually lost their interest in the boy and carried on with their merry business.

Well, almost all of the adults.

Barry suddenly felt a large hand grab onto his shoulder. The skin felt cold, almost freezing. He cocked an eyebrow and looked up behind him. Confusion etched itself into his face.

Nobody was there.

The hand let him go.

A cold patch was imprinted onto him.

"Weird," he commented before walking back over to his parents.

***

"Barry, wake up!"

The nineteen-year-old shook his head awake. He had dozed off in the driver's side seat, waiting for a representative to speak with him about sending a tow truck his way. "Hmm? I'm up, I'm up."

Sasha sighed as he stood over him. "We don't need you falling asleep, man. We want to get out of this desert sooner rather than later."

Barry rubbed his hazel eyes with his fingers. "I know, I know. These fuckers are taking their sweet time answering the phone."

"Are they even still on the phone?" Chelsea shouted from over Sasha's shoulder. "You sure they didn't hang up on your stupid ass while you were snoozing?"

The blonde glared at his best friend's girlfriend. "Yes. The classical music is still playing."

Sasha groaned. "Fuck. Is there a way you can leave a message for them? So, they can call back when they aren't getting swarmed by a bunch of idiot drivers who can't drive?"

Suddenly, the music stopped, and Barry's eyes widened. "Hello?! Is anyone there?!"

Much to his horror, the voice that spoke to him wasn't the one he wanted to hear. "*You're the fourth person in the queue. Your call is very important to us.*"

He threw his hand up. "What the hell?! It's been four god-damn people this whole time! What's so fucking dire that it trumps us being stuck in Death Valley?" He tossed the phone onto the ground, tempted to stamp the damn thing out.

"Don't you break your phone, Barry Waters," Chelsea ordered. "It's our only ticket out of this hellscape!"

Seething from hatred of the situation, Barry dropped onto the ground, laying in the sand. From the corner of his eye, he could see Rikki sitting on the other side of the car. She looked to be drawing a picture in the sand, though he couldn't see what it was from his angle. He was sure it was probably beautiful; much like her.

With a great sigh, Barry shook his head. "This is fucking bullshit," he muttered. "I never expected this to happen."

Sasha bent down and patted his shoulder. Barry instantly froze, terror rising up through his bloodstream. "We'll get out of this man," his best friend said. "Just you wait and see."

Barry's eye twitched. He was tempted to chew Sasha out for touching him, but he decided against it. He didn't know any better. He was only trying to be comforting. The blonde had no right to bite his head off.

"Y-Yeah. M-Maybe you're right."

The driver slid his arm over the sand, reaching for his phone. He grabbed it and pulled it back against his ear. The classical music was still playing.

"C'mon, he pleaded. "Please answer me. Please."

One minute passed and the sound of Bach was beginning to dig into the deepest crevices of his brain. Two minutes passed and Chelsea was sobbing loudly against Sasha's shoulder. Three minutes passed and the heat of the desert began to lessen. It was getting later in the day, meaning the heat would subside momentarily.

Good, Barry thought to himself. Maybe if, worst case scenario, he wasn't able to get an answer from anyone, the gang could spend the night under the cool desert sky. Would the heat pick up in the morning? Most likely, but at least they'd have some relief at long last.

After all, he didn't plan on staying in Death Valley forever.

"You're the fourth person in the queue. Your call is very important to us."

Chapter Four

Night Prowlers

The sun clocked out of his shift and was relieved by Lady Moon. She was in her waxing phase and shined brightly down upon the stranded college students. Barry stared up at her, admiring her in all of her majesty. It was a breath of fresh air after crashing his car and being unsuccessful at getting someone to help him and his crew out.

He'd given up on the tow truck by the time the sun set. It kept telling him he was the fourth caller in the queue, unchanging from that very number. Surely their system was down; why else would the same message repeat over and over again? Surely the three other callers ahead of him were just as impatient as he was. It was a miracle that he managed to stay on the phone for as long as he did without his battery dying!

His mother never called him back; a fact that weighed heavy on Barry's mind. Kathleen Waters was the biggest worrywart he'd ever met. If he didn't call her after a few days, she'd blow up his phone. "Are you alive?" she'd asked. "You haven't called in days. Are you sick? Hurt?"

Truth be told, he missed that level of worry right about now.

Her neuroticism was often annoying, but not now.

Not when there was an actual crisis.

Barry would've called his father, but the damn bastard hated technology. He could barely text, let alone answer a phone call! Gregory Waters was more of an old-fashioned man; landlines or nothing at all. "They're so much simpler," he'd argue. "They don't come with all the bells and whistles that these cell phones have!"

So calling his dad was out of the question.

No mother, no father, no tow truck.

Barry was truly terrified.

He breathed through his nose and slowly exhaled as he sat on the ground, leaning up against the front tire of the driver's side of the Chevy Malibu. "It'll be okay," he told himself in a raspy whisper. "We'll laugh about this at a Vegas casino. Or on the flight home. Or in class after Spring Break was over. Or perhaps never at all." At this point, Barry didn't care one way or another; so long as he could get the hell out of Death Valley.

At the present moment, Sasha and Chelsea were asleep in the back seat of the car. Rikki hadn't moved from her spot adjacent to Barry. Given that they were going to be stuck in the desert all night, Barry figured perhaps he could pass the time by talking to the attractive red head. That is, if she wasn't mad at him for wrecking the car.

How was he supposed to know a large dog was going to appear out of thin air? He still had a hard time even believing that he'd hit one! There was no body anywhere and no trail of blood. Of course, Barry had to wonder what exactly *did* he hit. The ground was smooth, no signs of obstruction in sight!

This hadn't been the first time that he'd experienced something that was unexplainable. It probably wouldn't be the last, either. But when something weird enough to destroy his car occurred, that's when the blonde became bitter and full of resentment. He closed his eyes, slowly blinking.

He was getting tired.

But he wanted to speak with Rikki.

This might've been the only opportunity that they could talk.

So, Barry stood up and walked over to the passenger side of the totaled vehicle. Upon first sight, he saw that Rikki had drawn a full mural into the sand. There was a winged man flying up to the sun, surrounded by doves.

"Is that Icarus?" he asked, making her jump just a little. "It kind of reminds of that story."

She looked at him and smiled nervously. "Y-Yeah. The story of Icarus has always been a favorite of mine."

"Is that so?" Barry said, crossing his arms. "You're into Greek Mythology?"

Rikki nodded. "You can say that I guess. I find it all very fascinating," she stretched her arms, her joints popping. "Like Icarus, for instance. He was warned about flying too close to the sun and died because of it."

Barry snorted, now leaning against the car. "Play stupid games, win stupid prizes."

"Yeah," she said with a slow nod. "You can say that again."

The blonde forced a chuckle. "So, what draws you toward that story, if I may ask?"

The red head shrugged. "I guess it's a humbling tale. It teaches a lesson in humility. We're all on Earth together. There may be other planets in our solar system, but we're the only ones here right now. Thinking you're better than everyone else will just get you killed because of foolish pride aiming to boost the cloud your judgment."

Barry nodded.

He loved a woman with insight.

"So, you're saying that Icarus teaches us to not be too cocky, lest it does us in."

Rikki smiled, which made the blonde grin. "Exactly."

The young man ran a hand through his mid-length hair. "So, you draw?"

The woman scratched the back of her neck. "Yeah. I always draw whenever I'm nervous or scared."

Barry frowned. She was probably angry with him for putting everyone in this predicament. Had he paid attention to the road, he wouldn't have wrecked the car. He wouldn't be stuck in uncharted territory.

"I'm scared too," he admitted. "I don't like being stranded."

Rikki chuckled nervously. "Who *does* like it?"

"Fair point," he said with a fake laugh. If he played his cards right, he'd be able to get her in bed with him. Maybe not at the present moment, but eventually. Perhaps when they were in their Vegas hotel room.

"How much water do we have left?" Rikki asked casually.

Barry tried to think for a moment, holding his index finger up. When he couldn't remember, he rushed over to the back of his car. He opened up. In order to count the bottles, he needed to weed through the empty bottles that everyone had been tossing into the trunk.

"Let's see," Barry murmured, raising his voice to count aloud. "One, two, three, for, five six...ten."

Rikki frowned at the blonde. "As much as we've drank already, we don't stand much of a chance against this place."

Barry sighed. He wanted to argue with her, but he realistically knew he couldn't. They all had drunk through a few cases of water already. The one-hundred-nine-degree weather was killer on the skin; thank God the red head had sunscreen.

"We'll be okay," he decided as he closed the hood. "We'll be..."

Suddenly, a distraction caught Barry's attention from the back window of the Chevy Malibu. Inside the vehicle, Chelsea sat on her knees, which were cushioned in the back seat. She was bobbing her head back and forth into Sasha's crotch.

"Hey!" Barry called out, slamming his hand into the back window. "Don't do that in my car!" The loving couple didn't hear him, or simply chose to ignore him. So he beat his hand into the back of the window again.

"Stop! No fucking in my car!"

His outburst managed to grab Sasha's attention, who instantly pushed Chelsea off him and zipped up his pants. "Fuck off, Barry," Chelsea said, voice muffled through the window. "This isn't your car anymore."

"Yes, it is!" Barry argued. "Just because it's wrecked doesn't mean it isn't my car."

Suddenly, Rikki quickly stood up and walked a little way from the car. The blonde immediately noticed and stepped away from the lovers. "What's up?"

Rikki looked back at Barry and pointed forward. "Listen," the man did as he was told, hearing nothing but birds in the distance. "You hear that?"

Barry cocked an eyebrow. "I hear birds, if that's what you're talking about."

"No," she whispered. "I'm not talking about birds."

Barry listened closely, trying to see if he heard anything else that sounded eerie or strange. Sadly, no sort of sound was heard. "Rikki, I don't hear anything."

The red head looked at him in disbelief. "How could you not? It's so loud. Sounds like wisps of wind trying to speak."

"Wind?" Barry asked, squinting at the woman. "There's not the slightest hint of a breeze right now. It's chilly, though."

Rikki frowned, turning back to face the nothingness ahead of her. "I hear it, though."

Barry stared uncomfortably at the young woman. Was she crazy? Was the type to heard voices in her head? He wouldn't have protested, but it was certainly disturbing him.

Then again, Chelsea swore up and down that Barry hit a large dog, so perhaps he was the schizophrenic one.

"You said it's trying to talk?" he asked nervously. "What's it saying?"

Rikki listened in for another moment, eventually shaking her head. "I don't know. It's garbled up."

Barry nodded slowly. "At least it's nothing sinister, right?"

Chapter Five

115 Degrees

Barry didn't get any sleep that night. Too much anxiety rested within his brain and heart. Lots of what-ifs plagued his mind. What if they never escaped the desert? What if they died from heatstroke or dehydration?

What didn't help was the temperature spike once the sun arose from his slumber. It had gone from eighty-four degrees to one-hundred-fifteen degrees. Barry knew this because his cell phone threw up an overheating warning within an hour after everyone else woke up. Sasha and Chelsea slept in the car and Rikki slept on the cool sandy ground.

By noon, Barry was drenched in sweat. Body odor seeped from his armpits and balls. But that was okay because everyone else was also stinking pretty badly. If only there were a river nearby; he could bathe and find sweet relief from the hot sun.

Leaning up beside the driver's side of the Chevy Malibu, Barry grasped his water bottle. He'd already drank most of it, save for about four ounces. Initally, the plan was to drink sparingly so it would last him until nightfall. But that's not what happened; the hot sun made damn sure of that.

"Well, screw me," Barry muttered as he chugged the remaining fluid from the bottle. Once he swallowed, he crushed the plastic and tossed it far into the desert. With a sigh, the young man pushed himself off the scorching hot car. It felt like hot coals were burning on his back, but what else could he lean on? A cactus? As much as he liked Rikki, he couldn't bring himself to so much as to graze her shoulder in the car.

At this point, it was a miracle that he hadn't developed sun poisoning.

Or perhaps he did, and he just didn't notice?

Was that even possible, he wondered.

The car felt like the fires of Hell at first, but Barry grew acclimated to the feeling once he'd leaned on it for longer than a few seconds. It really only hurt when he first touched it and when he stepped away. "Roasting like a fucking bird out here," the blonde muttered to himself. "Not even sunscreen seems to help. Surprised I haven't just caught on fire."

Meanwhile, inside the car, Sasha held his half-empty water bottle against his neck. Barry didn't understand why he was doing that. The H2O certainly wasn't cool enough to provide any sort of relief to his skin; that was a fact Barry was absolutely sure of. And as Sasha switched sides, he grew ever more frustrated.

"Why can't water just, I don't know, stay cold?"

Rikki, who had been leaning her head against the headrest in the passenger seat, fanned herself with both of her hands; a fruitless endeavor, to be sure. But Barry couldn't blame a girl for trying. "Everlasting cold wouldn't be possible in this heat. Even if you had an ice pack, it would certainly melt within a few hours."

Sasha snorted. "Thanks, Debbie Downer. For your information, any amount of cold would be preferable; regardless of how long it lasts."

Chelsea, who had been sucking on a lit cigarette, sat beside her man and pondered. "Is this what dying feels like? I think I'm dying."

Sasha pointed at her lung killer. "If you keep smoking those, you will die."

"Not what I meant, asshole," she snapped. "I don't have to spell out what I meant for you. You're a smart guy; you can figure it out yourself."

Rikki looked over at Chelsea through the rear-view mirror. "Don't be so hard on him. You're still breathing. We aren't dead until we stop."

The streaked woman rolled her eyes. "No shit, Captain Obvious. But how long until we stop breathing? I can hardly breathe with this temperature," she sniffled, on the verge of tears. "I'm saying we're all going to die out here."

Barry heard the conversation at hand, but he didn't chime in with his two cents. He was nearly at his limit with Chelsea.

She was a bitch who did nothing but complain. She obviously was a good lay, because there's no other reason Sasha would put up with her.

Oh well, Barry thought to himself.

He'd hold his tongue for his best friend's sake; regardless of how thin his patience had worn.

One ear, out the other.

"Don't say that," Sasha pleaded. "You need to have some faith. I'm praying every second that someone saves us."

Chelsea exhaled smoke outside her window. "Since when have you been a praying man?"

"I will make an exception this one time," he explained. "Why don't you?"

Tossing her cigarette out into the desert, Chelsea turned to glare daggers through her boyfriend. "Because we're screwed. Fuckface Waters can't get a hold of anyone and none of our phones work out here. The car is totalled; it won't even start long enough for us to run the AC. What are we going to do, Sasha? You tell me!"

Sasha angrily tossed the water bottle into the dashboard, making Rikki jump. "I don't know, okay?! I have no fucking clue how we're going to get out of this!"

Having had enough of the lover's quarrel, Rikki stepped outside the car and walked toward the trunk so the couple wouldn't see her. Much to Barry's delight, she pulled her green top off and dropped it to the ground. Her chest was well-endowed, Barry noticed. They looked full within her beige bra.

Following her example, Barry removed his own t-shirt, dropping it beside his feet. He wasn't a fat man, but he did have a little pudge in his gut. It ran in his family on his father's side. All of the males had dad bods, meaning Barry was doomed to follow the same fate within a few years.

If he lived that long.

Riding off the momentum from last night, he stepped over toward her. He hoped she'd notice his chest and fawn over him; lord knew he was fawning over her chest.

"They're annoying. I get it."

Rikki pushed her hands into her lower back, stretching.

Was she doing this on purpose?

Was she trying to tempt the young man?

"They're a bit much," she said quietly. "Though I can't blame Chelsea for being worried."

Barry sighed. "Yeah, I know."

Rikki looked down at her feet. "I can't stop thinking about last night. That weird noise I heard, but you didn't. It's bizarre."

"Yeah," he said with a quick nod. "You're right. It is bizarre."

Taking a deep breath, she slowly looked back up at Barry. "You don't suppose it was a spirit, do you?"

His eyes widened. "Why do you say that?"

"I don't know," she said, shaking her head. "It just felt like something was trying to tell me something," she tilted her head to the right. "Do you believe in the supernatural, Barry?"

Yes.

Yes, he did.

He refused to divulge that information, however.

She wouldn't believe him, no matter how superstitious she was.

"Nah. I think it's all bullshit."

Rikki frowned. "That's a shame. If only more people believed. Then wc could open our minds to the mysteries of the spirit world."

Suddenly, Rikki's eyes widened and she turned away from Barry.

"What's wrong?" he asked.

"I hear it again," she explained. "I can hear it speaking."

Barry's forehead wrinkled. "What is it saying?"

She held her right index finger up, listening in. After a long couple of seconds, she started running further into Death Valley. "Hey!" he called out. "We should stay together so nobody gets lost!" Alas, the red head didn't hear him, or maybe she simply chose not to acknowledge his words. "*Rikki*?!"

Barry hurried after her into the throes of Death Valley. Heatwaves hit him directly in the face, disorienting him. "R-Rikki..." he called out weakly. "Don't go." The blonde dropped to his knees as his vision began to swirl like a vortex. He then hunched over and hurled the contents of his stomach out onto the burning sand.

Gagging at the taste of bile in his mouth, Barry felt his limbs tremble. Was Chelsea right? Were they going to die in this desert? Black spots began to flash before his eyes.

This is it, he thought to himself.

"I-I'm done for," he muttered just before falling face-first into the burning sand.

***

"Honey, wake up," his mother urged with a gentle nudge on the child's shoulder. "It's time for the complimentary breakfast downstairs."

Young Barry opened his eyes and gave his arms and legs a good stretch. The queen-sized bed was oh-so-comfortable; he didn't want to crawl out just yet. Breakfast could wait, right? "Gimme five more minutes," he pleaded.

Then, from out of nowhere, Barry's dad scooped him out of bed, carrying him fireman style. "Okay, Sport. We're hungry, so you need to get up."

Caught by surprised, Barry wiggled around in his father's arms. "H-Hey! Put me down, Dad!"

Gregory Waters laughed, putting him down so his feet were touching the floor. "Alright, Son. Get dressed; I hear there's shrimp downstairs."

Barry's eyes lit up. "Let's go, let's go!"

"Get dressed first, Barry," his mother commanded. Doing as he was told; the boy grabbed a handful of clothes from out of his bag and rushed into the bathroom. Within a few minutes, Barry emerged, dressed in a blue t-shirt and red shorts.

"Ready?" Kathleen asked.

The boy nodded.

"Alright, let's go get some shrimp."

His parents stepped toward the door of their hotel room. The blonde child followed but was suddenly stopped in his tracks. A cold breeze suddenly blew onto his arms. He thought maybe it was just the air conditioner. But he was wrong.

A presence grabbed him by his shoulders.

It pulled him back into the bathroom.

The boy screamed.

"Help!"

Kathleen and Gregory quickly turned around and hurried toward the child as he fell over on his back. "Barry?! What's wrong?!"

Barry quickly sat up and looked behind him. His breathing quickened. "What the?!"

Before his eyes was nothing.

No person nor creature.

Just nothing at all.

"What is it, son?!" his dad asked.

The boy huffed and puffed, still looking at the nothingness that stood before him. "I-I got pulled back! Something grabbed me!"

The parents looked at each other, perplexed. "Barry," Kathleen said quietly. "Nothing grabbed you. We'd know if it did."

"Yeah," said Gregory. "You just tripped was all. Now come on; let's eat." The parents continued their trek into the hallway.

Barry's heart sank.

He had a very scary feeling; like something wasn't right.

Chapter Six

120 Degrees

A splash of water jolted Barry away from his comatose state. The liquid was warm like heated milk; the combination of cumulative sweat and warm water emulated the smell of a football team's locker room. The loss of perspiration was beginning to take its toll on the blonde. It was taking its toll on everyone else, too.

Barry shook his head, gasping for air. "W-Wha--"

"Shut up, man," Sasha urged his friend. "You're very sick," he reached for the full water bottle in Chelsea's hand, as she was standing directly behind him. "Drink up."

Wasting no time, the blonde man yanked the bottle from Sasha's hand and downed every drop in one large gulp. Once he was finished, he dropped the empty plastic beside him on the floorboard of his Chevy Malibu. He then slowly sat up to observe his surroundings. Even sitting up as slowly as he did, his head began to hurt.

"Ugh," he groaned. "I think I'm going to be sick."

"Please don't," Sasha pleaded. "Then I'll have to rag on you for the rest of your life."

Barry smirked. "You'd rag on me for being sick? Bastard."

Sasha forced a wide grin. "Hey, if you throw up in the car, I think we're all going to kick your ass. Nobody wants that smell lingering."

"Our body odor is any better?" Barry inquired. "Because we all are beyond the point of reeking like..." The sweat running down his back felt like molten hot lava. His eyes widened and he yelped. "*Fuck*!"

How his body ached.

How his skin burned.

How was he, or anyone else for that matter, still alive?

"Do we have any more sunscreen?" he inquired with a gasp.

Sasha frowned. "No. We used the last bit on you."

Barry bit his bottom lip, trying not to hyperventilate. The now scantily clad nurses that were Sasha and Chelsea watched the blonde, making sure he wasn't about to keel over. Rikki, on the other hand, had returned to the car. Much like the other three students, her skin was beet red. Her eyes were shut, suggesting she was either asleep or in need of immediate medical attention.

At this point, Barry was sure the trip to Vegas would be

largely spent in the ER...if they managed to make it to Vegas. "W-What happened?" he asked, looking at the red head as his hands shook.

Chelsea shoved Sasha aside to glare at the downed man. "You and your girlfriend ran out into the desert like a bunch of dumbasses, that's what happened. What the hell were you thinking?"

For once, Barry was thankful that his skin was as red as a to-mato; otherwise, they'd see him blushing over the "girlfriend" comment. He knew Chelsea was just being facetious, but still. Now wasn't the time for being facetious, nor was it the time to fawn over some girl. Lives were at stake. Barry needed to keep his head together.

"I-I was thinking that something had Rikki spooked, because she ran out into the desert first," he explained, now looking at the streaked girl. "I went to go check up on her and, next thing I knew, I was getting very sick and passed out."

Chelsea scoffed at his answer. "Well, that was awfully stupid of you. You had us all worried, motherfucker."

Barry chuckled weakly.

If he didn't know any better, he'd say the bitch actually had a soft spot for him.

"And you," she said, expression softening as she addressed Rikki. "Girl, you know better than to scare everyone by running out into the desert. What happened?"

The blonde cocked an eyebrow. Chelsea was showing an

awful lot of concern for them. He was surprised to see her be nice for a change. Not very nice, of course. But better than usual.

"I'm sorry," Rikki mumbled quietly. "I just...heard something. Something awful. I was scared."

"What was it?" Sasha asked, nudging Chelsea aside. "Was it something feral like a coyote? Something otherworldly like a UFO beam?"

Chelsea squinted at him.

"What?" he asked, looking as her. "I've heard about alien sightings in Death Valley. I'm not just pulling this out of my ass!"

Rikki opened her eyes. "I heard music."

The streaked girl nodded slowly. "Okay, you're obviously delirious. Hearing random music out in a barren desert isn't normal."

Barry snorted. "Seeing imaginary dogs out in a barren desert isn't normal, either."

"It wasn't imaginary!" Chelsea growled. "I saw it! What else could've possibly wrecked your car?!"

Suddenly, the faint sound of sobbing distracted the bickering students. They both looked over at Rikki, who had tears rolling down her cheeks. Barry's expression softened. "Rikki?" At the sound of her name, the waterworks exploded out of her like a bomb.

Barry's heart ached.

He always hated seeing women cry.

He was raised to be gentle, not a burden.

A gentleman.

"I heard a song, okay?!" Rikki cried.

Sasha cocked an eyebrow. "How is that awful? Was it a terrible song?"

Rikki shook her head. "T-The song isn't terrible. But the memories associated with it hurt so much that I can't stand it."

"What kind of music was it?" Barry asked.

The red head's shook as she recollected on her past. "Y-You are the dancing queen. Young and sweet, only seventeen..."

Chelsea made a sound that signified confusion. "*That's* what you heard? That old song from the seventies? What's so terrible about that, other than it being ancient?"

Rikki swallowed an incoming breath and closed her eyes again. Memory lane awaited her with pitchforks and torches.

***

Being a trained ballet dancer gave the seventeen-year-old an edge over the other contestants. Did that mean they were terrible? Not by any stretch of the imagination. Every single girl and boy in that competition was a dancer worthy of recognition.

But Rikki Simmons was different.

She was born to dance.

It's all she wanted to do with her life.

Sure, she was talented with a paintbrush. She's even been told that she had potential to become a well-renowned artist, should she work hard to further develop her artistic skills. However, there was no money to be made doing art for a living. Not that it was a phony field of work, but they were called starving artists for a reason.

Dancing, though? She could've easily been hired to appear in a music video or several. Maybe she'd be considered to dance on Broadway! Rikki could win championships, awe adoring fans, and relish every moment of her life doing what she loved.

To kickstart her career, she made it to a national dance competition in Boston, Massachusetts. The teenager had always wanted to visit the state of Massachusetts. Boston was such a bustling city full of fascinating sights. But she really wanted to visit Salem and explore the controversial history of the town.

But one thing at a time, she told herself.

For now, she had a competition to win.

Rikki remembered her nerves spiking as the girl before her was going crazy on stage with her interpretative dance routine to Pink Floyd's "Comfortably Numb". The way she moved was mesmerizing. Her movements captivated the audience with how graceful they were.

People often said dance can move people to tears. Rikki certainly believed that statement, as she was certainly moved. Everything about the raven-haired, mulatto skinned girl from Indianapolis was beautiful. The red head greatly envied her. She'd really have to up the ante if she wanted to beat her.

Her heart raced as the performance came to an end. The standing ovation shook the entire auditorium and Rikki felt herself at a disadvantage. Yes, she was a fantastic dancer. But could she possibly compare to this majestic mistress who just rocked the whole house?

"Keep it together," she muttered to herself. "You got this."

The other dancer stepped off stage and passed by Rikki, offering her a smile. "Good luck!"

The red head wanted to verbally thank her, but she could only bring herself to nod in acknowledgement. The fluttering in her stomach was making her nauseous and she really didn't want to puke all over the stage; so it was best to keep her mouth shut.

Once the competition was ready for her, the middle-aged female host spoke to the crowd. "Okay ladies and gentlemen, put your hands together for our next contestant. From Wilkes-Barre, Pennslyvania, give it up for Miss Rikki Simmons!"

The host's voice sent shivers down the teenager's spine. This was it, the moment of truth. The chance for her to truly shine was upon her. Was she ready?

The audience clapped and Rikki hurried onto the stage. And in an instant, as she stared down the eager crowd, he felt her anxiety wash away. The seventeen-year-old became the poised professional that she knew herself to be. As the spotlight shined upon her, she was ready to put on the show of a lifetime.

The beginning of ABBA's "Dancing Queen" erupted from the speakers. Rikki bounced on her heels to the beat of the music, allowing the vocals to start before letting loose.

"You can dance! You can jive! Having the time of your life!"

Rikki spun herself around, moving her arms in an elegant, but fun rhythm to match the tone of the song.

"See that girl! Watch that scene! Digging the dancing queen!"

The red head used her ballet training to skillfully balance her- self on her tiptoes as she maintained a steady pattern of move- ment. She bobbed her arms in synchronicity with the vocals. Her hips swayed, and she lost herself to the dance. The audience seemed to love her, as they cheered loudly as she stretched and gyrated.

All was going well until it wasn't.

The lights suddenly went out, but the music remained. Blood-curdling screams echoed throughout the auditorium. Rikki stopped dancing in the attempt to see what was going on.

Within a few moments, the screaming stopped and the lights over the crowd came back on.

"You are the dancing queen!"

Her jaw dropped.

"Young and sweet, only seventeen!"

Rikki screamed loudly at the sight before her. The audience members, including her father and kid sister, were all sprawled out in their seats and the floor. Puddles of blood soaked the marble floor and lacerations presented themselves proudly on the necks of a couple of people. Some people even had their entrails falling out of their gutted stomachs.

Her father was lying face-first on the floor, blood circled around him.

Her sister's throat was slashed.

The smell of rotting flesh permeated in her nostrils.

Everyone was dead.

"No! No!"

"See that girl! Watch that scene! Digging the dancing queen!"

The more frantic her screams became the less balance she had. She fell onto her ass, now covering her mouth and nose to save herself from the horrible smell. "Keeyee," she said in a muffled voice, trying to say her sister, Kayla's, name. "Dayee!" The word "Daddy" bounced off her sweaty palm.

And within a flash, her spotlight came back on.

Everyone was back to normal.

No lacerations, no entrails, no blood.

Even her father and sister were okay, albeit horrified at the show she'd put on for everybody.

It was as if nothing happened to them.

But it was so real to Rikki.

The entire auditorium stared at her in disbelief, feeling the secondhand mortification the dancer was experiencing. ABBA's song finally concluded, leaving everyone in silence. Desperate to get away from the nightmare, Rikki quickly stood up and sprinted backstage.

Her dreams of being a dancer were over. The audience was gone, the show had ended. She decided to pursue a degree in art as a hail Mary. The vibrance of her character that shined in her dance was no more.

Painting heathers and Greek legends were all she had left anymore.

***

Rikki slowly opened her eyes and looked up into the rearview mirror. "I can't say. I just...I just can't say. Please understand."

Barry felt himself conflicted. On one hand, he wanted to understand what she had been through and respected her wishes not to divulge any further. But, on the other hand, he felt anger. Why couldn't she tell them what was going on? Something fishy was going on in Death Valley and he needed context so he could better understand.

Chelsea's dog.

Rikki's whispers and music.

Permanent hold with the tow truck service.

His parents' silence.

"Can you please tell us? Rikki?" he asked with a tinge of frustration. "If you tell us, we might be able to better figure out why things are so weird around here."

Rikki shook her head. "Barry, please. Don't make me tell the story. It hurts too much."

Barry's expression went from soft to hard and cold. "Your feelings can't matter more when our lives are at stake."

"Dude," Sasha said, touching his arm. "Let it go."

Feeling the unwanted touch was the final straw. Barry reared back and punched Sasha in the face, knocking him to the ground. "Don't fucking touch me!" He tugged at his hair frantically. "Water. I need more water."

Chelsea, who had crouched down to check on her man, looked up at Barry not with anger, but worry. "Barry, you drank the last bottle. There's no more water."

His eyes widened. "What do you mean there's no more water?!"

"Exactly what I said," she concurred. "Maybe we can get some from a cactus or something."

Barry bit his bottom lip hard enough to draw blood before storming off in a panic. "Fuck, fuck, fuck!" They were now at the mercy of the one-hundred-twenty-degree weather. No water, no hope.

Chapter Seven

Darkness

As night fell, Barry found it hard to count his blessings. He'd lost his temper. He hurt his group with his actions. He made himself look like a trainwreck.

He was still alive somehow. How did he manage that? How did anyone manage that? If it were anyone else, they would've died the first day. What made his group so special?

Despite the poor condition of their bodies, they'd all managed to cheat death for now. Heat poisoning was the last thing they should've worried about, Barry decided. There was still no sign of a saving grace coming their way. The tow truck hotline was useless and his mother still hadn't called him back.

So he decided to give her another ring.

He picked her number from his speed dial list and held the phone up to his ear. "Please, Mom. Please answer." The first ring passed, then the second. By the time the third ring had passed, Barry began to seethe.

"This is Kathleen Waters. I am unavailable at the moment. Please leave your name and number and I'll get back with you shortly. Okay bye!"

Barry felt hot tears roll down his face as the beep after the voicemail message sounded. "Mom, please call me. Please! We're stranded in Death Valley. No water, no food, no air-conditioning, no car," he sobbed loudly. "Please, Mom. I need your help," suddenly, his tone abruptly changed. "Why aren't you answering me, you fucking bitch? Do you want me to die out here? Well, you better be lucky you aren't here with me. Because I will gut you like a fucking fish and feast on your intestines. You think I'm lying, you worthless cunt? Fucking try me."

He ended the call and chucked his phone far out into the desert. What was the point of keeping it? The battery was going to die soon, anyway. Plus, it was pretty fucked up that the crew designated him to be the savior with the operational phone.

He made a decision at that moment.

He decided that his "friends" deserved his wrath.

They were all worthless to him.

Barry collapsed onto the ground. The sand was cold, but his body still screamed at him. The perpetual feeling of hot coals burning all over him was driving him noticably insane. He began to to permanently see black spots floating before his eyes. Even in the darkness of the night, the spots wouldn't go away.

Sometimes they'd form into shapes. The most elaborate of all was a shadowy gazelle, happily prancing through the lonely desert. Within this creature, Barry found a friend; better a friend than any of the chucklefucks loafing around his deceased ride.

How Barry wished to join the gazelle. He wished he could be a hallucination, too. He wouldn't feel any more pain. He wouldn't feel anymore fear. He wouldn't exist at all.

It was true; Barry felt his grasp on reality slipping away. His altercation was the second to last straw to break the camel's back. His failed phone call to his mother was the final one.

Tears streamed down his face as he turned to look at his crew. Sasha and Chelsea were sitting on the ground together, his arm around her. Barry sniffled for a moment, his eyes gradually turning into an icy glare.

How could those two be so lovey-dovey during a time like this? Didn't they realize the gravity of their situation? They should've been trying to help Barry find a way out. Instead, they just complained all the time. Sasha was a pussy-whipped bitch and Chelsea was a hateful cunt.

And then there's Rikki Simmons. What a fucking *angel* she was. She had the gall to not tell anyone about her past. What made her so entitled to keep important information to herself? Did she want him to die?

Barry smiled as he pictured himself knocking her onto the ground, breaking her neck, and then fucking her skull. Just her screaming, begging him not to kill her. But he'd do it anyway.

She had her chance to be useful. She decided against it, so what was the point of keeping her alive?

As far as he was concerned, the slut was going to rot in the fucking desert and serve as grub for the buzzards.

He wasn't going to waste any more time considering her feelings.

As he coldly stared at his "friends", he noticed Sasha's head suddenly pop up. The brunette's eyes were widened. "What was that?!" he shouted. "Anyone else hear that?!"

Chelsea looked around. "Hear what?"

Sasha stood up and frantically looked around. "Who the fuck is saying that?! What would you know about my football days, you motherfucker?!"

Now Chelsea was standing up. She grabbed onto her man's arm. "Nobody is saying a goddamn thing, you psycho!"

At the word "psycho", Sasha punched her in the face.

She recoiled and then slapped him hard.

Before Barry knew it, the lovely couple was tackling each other on the ground. They wailed on each other as Rikki ignored them, stargazing like the useless bitch she was.

Barry smiled wide. Good girl, he thought to himself. Instead of skull-fucking her, he'd just force himself on her over his car; screams be damned.

The blonde watched with envy. How he wished he could be the one making mincemeat out of Sasha's face. How he hated his best friend and his whore. How he hated Rikki.

A whisper crawled into his ear like a tiny ant sneaking into a picnic. "*You're alive because I will it,*" it said, gender fairly ambiguous. "*You're my God. You deserve to live.*"

Barry looked up at the moon, eyes wide and pupils dilated.

He had finally succumbed to the madness.

Chapter Eight

The Star

"It's not often that freshmen make quarterback," said the rotund Coach Michael. As he looked at his clipboard, he rubbed his own bald head. "Adam Frehley is going to be upset that he was outshined by you."

Sasha Balandin grinned like an idiot. He was only five years old when his dad took him to see Super Bowl XLIV. "I don't understand American Football," he commented with his thick Russian accent. "So maybe seeing teams face each other, I will grow to have an appreciation for the sport."

It had been the New Orleans Saints and the Indianapolis Colts facing off. Sasha's American mother insisted that his dad take him to Miami to see the game live. Lev Balandin was a financial analyst for Wall Street, so he was at work most of the time. Debra Balandin urged the boys to go spend some father-son time together.

And it was so worth it.

It had been Sasha's first time watching American Football and *he fell in love. He was too young to truly appreciate the strategical prowess of the teams, but he certainly enjoyed the rush of watching the surprise onside kick. It turned the game around for the Saints, and they ended up winning.*

The boy wanted to play football.

Not only were the players badass, they also made serious bank.

Multi-million contract to play for the NFL?

Sasha would've been stupid to not aspire to that!

His football career started in high school when he beat out Adam Frehley in the try-outs. Adam was an asshole junior with a big head on his shoulders. When he wasn't being a creep to all the cheerleaders, he was bullying nerds. He was a stereotypical jock and Sasha felt secondhand embarrassment for the stupid bastard. It had to be hard to be a real-life cartoon character.

"To tell you the truth Coach? I could give a rat's ass about Adam Frehley. I'm the better player. I deserve to be on the team; he's had his time to shine for two damn years. Let the new guy come in, you know?"

The black man smirked. "I like you, Balandin. You got balls. I need more players like you on the team," he squinted at the freshman. "Just don't get too cocky, alright? That's how players get afflicted with career-ending injuries."

Sasha nodded. "Message received, but I know what I'm doing. I've been training for years. I'm ready to play for a team."

Coach Michael patted his shoulder. "Welcome to the Seagulls, Balandin."

The fourteen-year-old glowed for the rest of the day. The urge to brag about his QB status was very strong; especially to Adam Frehley. But for now, he had someone else to impress. And that person was much more attractive than Adam could ever hope to be.

Chelsea Franks.

Back then, she had short hair, dyed purple. She hung around the alternative crowd; smoking cigarettes in the parking lot, ditching class, and getting into fights. She was a badass bitch and her attitude turned him on. It could also be because she was the closest thing to a big titty goth girl; either or was a possibility.

Would she be impressed by him making QB? Probably not. If anything, she'd call him a pig-headed jock. But that was okay, because he had the ultimate plan to gain her affection.

He was going to bring a large sign to his first game which would read "Date Me, Chelsea Franks!!". Was it desperate? Maybe. But his dad always told him ladies loved sappy romance. So that's precisely what he was going to do.

Come lunch time, Sasha carried his tray to the table that his buddies chose to sit at that day. They often sat front and center, but that day they were strategically seated in the back left corner where the alternative kids sat. Sasha's friends knew he liked Chelsea, so they decided to celebrate him making QB by giving him an opportunity to make smooth moves on the lady.

If he failed, oh well. Ladies loved confidence, so he maintained utmost confidence in himself.

"Yo, Quarterback!" called Preston Derek, his friend since seventh grade. "Get your ass over here!"

With a big smile, Sasha made his way to the table. He appreciated Preston calling for him as loudly as he could; it was sure to get Chelsea's attention one way or another. Sasha sat beside Preston and his other buddy, Gary Cord. Gary was, for a lack of better word, a dweeb. But he had the funniest stories to tell. His sense of humor was unmatched, and Sasha adored him for it.

"You aren't going to stuff me in a locker, are you?" Gary asked as Sasha sat himself down with his lunch tray. "Because I have pepper spray, fucker."

Sasha chuckled. "Only on Game Day. Gotta maintain a reputation, you know?"

Gary snorted. "So, you've chosen mace to the face. Got it."

Sasha glanced over at Chelsea, who paid no mind whatsoever to him. "You know you gotta talk to her, right?" Preston said, egging the QB on. "She's not just going to throw herself at your feet just because you're a big sports star now."

The QB sighed. "Yeah, I know. I'm just trying to think of a conversation piece that isn't related to football."

"But women love watching guys slap each other on the ass!" Gary commented. "It gets them horny when their man loves dick more than they do."

Sasha sighed. "No. I need to be more interesting than that."

He knew nothing about Chelsea at that point, other than she was a lovable bitch who smoked cigarettes. Maybe he could do that? Talk about cigarettes. It was worth a shot.

So the QB stood up and strutted confidently to Chelsea's table. The alternative kids were talking to each other in gravely voices about God knows what. Sasha cleared his through, getting the attention of the crew.

"Hello, friends! Did you know that tobacco originated in Mayan culture?"

They all looked at him with disinterest.

Chelsea quietly munched on a slice of thin crust pizza as she awkwardly stared at him.

"Good talk," Sasha said, still maintaining his air of confidence. he retreated to go sit with his friends again. Gary was laughing his ass off. "Oh boy! You struck out hard. Tobacco? That's the best you could come up with?!"

Sasha punched him in the arm. Before he could say anything else, he saw a hulking goliath stomping his way. It was none other than Adam Frehley, looking especially angry. "Hey Pussy!" Once he made it to the table, he took Sasha's tray and tossed it into the wall, splattering his sloppy joe all over the place. "You got me demoted to fucking linebacker!"

Sasha shrugged, trying to play it cool. "Sucks to suck, Adam. Maybe you should've been a better player."

At those words, the former QB grabbed Sasha by the collar of his shirt and pulled him forward. "You're fucking dead!"

Luckily for Sasha, a teacher came to his aid, Mrs. Foster, the English teacher. "That's enough out of you boys! One more move like that and you're both suspended. Got it?!"

The new QB nodded. "Understood, ma'am." Adam, on the other hand, simply stormed off without a word. With a mischievous grin, Sasha sat back down. He looked back up at Chelsea, who looked to be smiling at him.

Mission accomplished!

One week passed by and Adam hadn't started anymore drama with Sasha. That night was Sasha's first game as QB. The game started rather unremarkably; team huddle, the opposing QB got sacked, cornerbacks were at their best, and Sasha managed to get a touchdown. The game was going well, it seemed.

But that was only the first quarter. By the time the second quarter came to be, Sasha was beginning to feel nervous. He had planned to ask Chelsea out during the game. But what if he just made a fool of himself with no payoff? No girlfriend to call his own?

He dared not put those negative thoughts into his head; he had a game to play.

Second quarter started off well enough; opposing team made a touchdown and the Seagulls' defense stepped it up. But there was a problem Sasha noticed; the linebackers were playing like shit. They weren't holding off anyone, they were just running around like chickens with their heads cut off.

"Time out," Sasha demanded, frustrated. The referee blew his whistle so the Seagulls could reconvene. Once the players huddled up, Sasha let loose. "Linebackers, what the hell are you doing out there? You did so well in the first quarter! What happened?"

Adam smirked. "Oh, nothing. Just that we found something that's got our side mighty pissed off," fishing into his pocket, he pulled out a piece of cardboard and handed it to Sasha.

The cardboard had a little red heart drawn on it...the same one he drew for his poster.

"You sonuvabitch," he growled.

"No," Adam argued. "You're the sonuvabitch. Cecil is Chelsea's brother. He doesn't take kindly to perverts lusting after his baby sister."

Cecil Franks, another large linebacker, stepped forward and cracked his knuckles. "Nice try, asshole. My sister isn't going to date someone like you."

Sasha bit his bottom lip. "You wanna fucking fight, dipshit? I'll happily oblige after the game is over."

Unfortunately, that wasn't an answer Cecil wanted to hear. He socked Sasha in the jaw, knocking him onto the grass and pushing the helmet off his head. The remaining players disbursed as Cecil climbed on top of Sasha and began choking him. Sasha gasped for air as the referee frantically blew his whistle in the attempt to stop the fight.

But Cecil wasn't listening. "I'm not going to let some freshman scumfuck touch my sister!"

Finally having enough, Sasha rolled them over, forcefully pulled his adversary's helmet off his skull, and began punching down on Cecil. The referee and Coach Michael pulled Sasha off him, but the Russian American was too pissed off to let it slide. He yanked away from Coach Michael and lunged at Cecil.

And then, as if time froze entirely, Sasha was free to wail on Cecil as much as he wanted. He had to have punched him at least thirty times before the bastard grew unconscious. Wanting to throw in one more punch, he socked him in the cheekbone.

But something horrible happened.

His fist went through Cecil's skin, breaking past his teeth. Sasha's eyes widened and he stepped away. Cecil Franks was dead. "Fuck, fuck, fuck, fuck, fuck..." Sasha removed his helmet and tossed it aside. "Cecil! Cecil, man! I'm so sorry! Please don't die on me!"

He looked at his hand, which was covered in blood and loose teeth. He screamed loudly, backing away from the corpse. He was a murderer. He needed to escape before the police arrived!

But then, by some miracle, Cecil sat up. His cheek was intact, as was his blood and teeth. The gunk on Sasha's hand disappeared. However, he seemed out of sorts due to the prior blows to his head. Cecil was taken to the ER that night, and Sasha never played football ever again.

Chapter Nine

125 Degrees

Her naked body burned under the scorching sun. Her skin was almost comically red, but she didn't seem to care anymore. She didn't even wear shoes to protect the pads underneath her feet. She hadn't a drop of sweat left in her body hardly, and even then, it seeped out of her pores and made her flesh glisten under the rays.

She was dying.

But she didn't care.

She just wanted to dance.

Barry enjoyed the show from within the car. He gripped the steering wheel tightly, fingers so tightly wrapped that his joints ached. What was new? His entire flesh suit of a body was in chronic pain. Joints on fire, skin on fire, bones weakening from within, internal organs struggling to function, and mind burnt to a crisp. He was barely functioning.

But that was okay.

He learned to give in and enjoy the agony.

Pain was the path of divinity, after all.

Being the deity he was, he knew he'd never die. It was the only explanation for why he hadn't keeled over in the inferno known as Death Valley. To be divine was both a blessing and curse. If only he could leave his current form and join the universe as an ethereal being once and for all.

As Barry watched Rikki, he noticed her mouth moving as if she were singing. However, no words came out; she was completely mute. That didn't bifront the blonde, of course. She had nothing of any particular relevance to say, anyway.

It was crazy. In another life, he had longed for her companionship. Her mind, body, and soul was beautiful and to be in her company made Barry feel blessed. How honorable to know Miss Rikki Simmons.

But that was a long time ago. She was now nothing more than a gorgeous meat puppet. Rikki was the Alcmene to his Zeus. She would be a good lay, but nothing more than that.

But if she wasn't majestic in her dance. How she seductively swayed her hips like a belly dancer. Watching her was equal parts titilating and infuriating. Curse his human body and its carnal urges!

Meanwhile, the loving couple behind Barry were both on the verge of death. Sasha was hunched over, crying frantically. Chelsea, on the other hand, looked to be caught in a dead stare with the back of Barry's headrest. Both of them were utterly pathetic, the blonde god thought to himself.

"I-I didn't mean to kill him," wailed the brunette. "He was trying to hurt me! He wouldn't let me be with the girl I love! What else was I supposed to do?!"

Chelsea sighed, speaking flatly and not taking her eyes off the headrest. "If you're talking about Cecil, he's not dead. He's alive and well."

Sasha turned to face his woman and grabbed a hold of her. He gave her a hard shake. "I know what I saw, Chelsea! Maybe you think he's alive, but that's only because his death hurt you so much! You're in denial!"

The streaked girl stared blankly into the abyss, not even reacting to her man's words with any emotion. "Okay."

Willing to intrude into the adorable conversation, Barry glared at Chelsea through the rearview mirror. "What the fuck are you staring at, anyway? I know it's an anomaly seeing beings like me in the flesh, but you need to stop staring."

Again, not reacting with any emotion, Chelsea continued to stare. "Okay."

Sasha looked at Barry, squinting. "Anomaly, Barry?"

"Yes," the blonde said pompously. "I don't expect your football brain to be capable of comprehending the meaning of that word."

Sasha shook, slowly raising an eyebrow. "I...I know what the word means, bro. The hell is wrong with you? I know tensions are high, but you're talking crazy."

Barry smiled widely. "There's nothing crazy about realizing one's true place in the universe. You'd do well to remember yours."

"What is that even supposed to mean?!" Sasha asked, shouting.

Before Barry could respond, Chelsea groaned loudly. "Water. I need water. T-There h-has to be a cactus nearby."

Her desperation made the blonde laugh manically. If she was that deprived of water, that meant she wasn't a god at all. Barry had began to worry that the other three were also divinity, given they hadn't croaked yet. He couldn't, and wouldn't, share the spotlight with any of these cretins.

"I'm dying," Chelsea finally admitted. "I h-hear her singing my death song. I hear Mom. I hear her wishing me good luck on the other side."

Barry's laughter slowly ceased, and he took a quick breath. "I could've told you that. You didn't need some old hag to tell you what everyone already knows."

Chelsea sniffled weakly. "I n-need water. Barry. Sasha. Please help me."

An evil grin crept over Barry's face. "Can you say that again?"

Another sniffle left the streaked girl. "Please help me."

Barry moaned with pleasure."Ummph, one more time!"

Chelsea shook her head. "Stop this, Barry. You're scaring me."

"Say it again, you stupid bitch," the blonde commanded. "Say it again or you'll fucking die in that goddamn seat."

Chelsea bit her bottom lip. If she were more hydrated, she'd probably shed a single tear. But she was incapable. All the water in her system had dried up.

"P-Please h-help me."

Satisfied with her compliance, Barry shook his head. "Yeah, no. Sorry, I don't feel like helping you at all."

Her eyebrows slowly rose. "Why not? I did what you asked."

"Yeah, man," Sasha chimed in. "What do you have to gain by letting my woman die?"

Barry chortled, finally letting go of the steering wheel. "I gain unmatchable power. You guys are holding me back. Once you're gone, I can leave this meaty sack of a body and join the sky as the one true God."

Sasha slowly shook his head. "You're...you're insane," Sasha stepped out of the vehicle. "I'm going to find water, if you won't."

Once Sasha hobbled off, Chelsea rose her severely shaking hands up to the headrest. "Barry, please. Don't let me die."

As much as the blonde enjoyed hearing her desperation, he knew he couldn't keep it up for too long until one of the idiots tried slaying him. Not that they would've succeeded, but he truly didn't feel up to a scuffle. He could stir the pot in many more ways that didn't have anything to do with fighting.

So, Barry eyeballed an empty plastic bottle in the passenger side floorboard. He leaned over to pick it up and then tossed it at Chelsea. "You know what to do."

The bottle landed in her lap as she stared blankly at the god. "No, I don't. This bottle is empty."

"So fill it up," Barry commanded. "Do it or you'll die. Choice is yours."

Finally connecting the dots, Chelsea squinted at the blonde god. "You're sick. I'm not drinking my own pee."

Barry shrugged. "Suit yourself. I guess you really want to die."

Chelsea dropped her hands to her lap. "Look Barry. I'm deeply sorry for all the times I was mean to you. And I don't apologize. I sincerely mean this from the bottom of my heart."

The blonde snorted. "Too little, too late. Now make your choice."

"Are you fucking serious right now?" she asked slowly. "You want me to pee in this bottle and drink it?"

Barry chuckled darkly. "You've placed your life in my hands.

You wanted me to go get you some water. Not Sasha, not Rikki. Me. And I say you either die like the skank you are, or you drink your own bodily essence. Either way, I'm in control."

Chelsea shook even harder now. "You're sick in the head. Delusional. You need serious psychiatric help."

Ignoring her words, Barry turned around in his seat. "Make your choice now. If yes, I will watch. If no, I'll mangle your fucking body like a frog in a high school science class."

Chelsea shivered and took the bottle. Waiting a short moment, she sighed. "I don't think I can do it. As dehydrated as I am--"

"Never say never," Barry said, growing impatient.

Chelsea stared at him for a moment before reluctantly reaching under her skirt to pull her panties down.

Chapter Ten

Behind Green Eyes

She was never good with apologies. She wasn't raised to say sorry; not like it would've helped her any, anyway. Living in the household she lived in; Chelsea Franks was both the bad guy and hardened martyr. Her mother made damn sure of that fact.

When Philip Franks walked out of Chelsea's life, things went downhill fast. Laura, her mother, went from a frustrated bitch to an aggressive monster. Her husband was having an affair with his co-worker; one that evolved from a simple fling to a marriage proposal. Chelsea wanted to think that he was a bad person for doing that to his family.

However, as she got to know the real Laura Franks, it all became very clear as to why he left.

The purple-haired girl often wondered if her father was ever beaten up by her mother. After all, she seemed to relish in caus-ing physical pain to her daughter. Such as the night where she chose to no-show the football game that her brother, Cecil, was competing in. She never had interest in the sport, so she didn't show up.

Alas, this angered Laura greatly.

"How dare you do this to your brother," she bellowed inside their newly renovated kitchen, still covered in saran wrap in a few spots. "We're a family! You must show support for your family, Chelsea!"

The teenager crossed her arms. "Cecil is seventeen. He's basically an adult at this point. If his feelings are hurt by his kid sister not attending the first game of the season, then maybe he needs counseling."

Her mother seethed as she punched Chelsea in the gut. The girl dropped to her knees, holding her stomach. "That's the last time you speak poorly about Cecil, you fucking wretch. If you can't show some respect in this household, then I have no wish to keep you under my roof."

Chelsea looked up Laura with an icy glare. "Look, I don't know why you blame me so much for Dad leaving. That's all this is about, right? You're still mad that--"

With an angry growl, her mother kicked her in the face. The girl fell back, her hand going up to feel her jaw. Surprisingly, it hadn't been broken that time. "I told you to never speak of that bastard in front of me ever again. I have to watch after two teen-agers while he's balls deep in some bimbo. He let his dick decide the fate of this family, Chelsea. I have every right to be angry!"

The teenager smirked while lying on the floor, trying to ignore the pain in her face and gut. "T-Technically, he decided the fate of this family when he got with you."

"Not what I meant!" Laure screeched. "You need to apologize to me right now, Chelsea. I've taken your abuse for far too long. While you're at it, apologize to your brother for being selfish."

The words wanted to come out for the sake of ending the violence. She wanted to say she was sorry for everything. She knew Dad leaving took its toll on her; it certainly took a toll on Chelsea and Cecil. But she could never bring herself to utter those three little words. Not like Laura truly deserved to hear them from her daughter, anyway.

"Apologize to me and I'll apologize to you," the teenage girl answered, sitting up. "This isn't a one-way street. You're wrong, too."

Laura bashed her fist into the wall. "I am not wrong. I'm not! You're just upset that you aren't important enough for Phillip to swing by and visit! None of us are! Why do you have to hurt me over it?"

"Hurt you?!" Chelsea squawked as she got back onto her feet. "I haven't laid the first hit on you!"

But then, in the nick of time, the sound of a car door shutting made its way to the women's ears. Cecil was home from the ER, driven home by his friend, Adam Frehley. Chelsea only knew this because Adam had called her from the ER, letting her know the general gist of what happened. He got in a fight and lost. What kind of linebacker could he possibly be if one fight was able to hurt him so much?

"This conversation is over," Laura decided. "Go to your room and think about what I said."

Utterly defeated, Chelsea stormed off to her room, livid about her lack of courage to simply clock the bitch right then and there. She could've just stayed put and defied her mother. She wouldn't have put on a smile for Cecil. She was sick of pretending to be okay.

Cecil would need to learn one day that Laura was a piece of shit. He was a big boy; he could handle it. Or perhaps he couldn't...he still hadn't gotten over his father's betrayal. In Cecil's mind, all men were pigs and his two women, Laura and Chelsea, needed to be protected at all times. Acquiring a boyfriend was impossible, as any guy who looked at Chelsea for longer than a few seconds was as good as dead. Her guy friends at school had to pretend to be gay, for God's sake!

Cecil needed to realize that not everyone who identified as a man was a total sleazeball. If they were, what did that make him? Last Chelsea had heard, her brother still considered himself a cisgender male. So that meant he was as sleazy and horny as the next guy, at least by his logic.

But women were delicate little flowers who must be regularly watered every day. Tender care and respect were all they needed to maintain a happy outlook on life. They were obviously dainty and frail, unable to defend themselves in a squabble. Never mind that Chelsea had proven time and time again that she was more than capable of kicking ass with barely a scratch on her.

But Cecil wouldn't hear it.

After all, who knew women better than men?

When her brother entered the house, Chelsea made a show

of stomping to her room in their two-story home in Queens. Her footsteps echoed throughout the house as she angrily climbed the stairs. "Wazz goin' on here?" Cecil asked aloud with a slurred voice, no doubt from the medication given to him at the hospital. The fourteen-year-old girl looked back, noticing that he had welts and bruises on his face. Damn, she thought to herself. He really did get a beating, didn't he?

But nevertheless, Chelsea hadn't the wherewithal to speak with him. So, she turned back and continued her trek up the stairs. "Oh, nothing is wrong," she heard her mother say. "She's just on her period. What's the verdict with you? Concussion? Any broken bones?"

Chelsea had slammed her door shut before she could hear her brother's answer. Surrounded by posters of punk rock bands, the purple-haired girl flopped onto her bed and buried her face into her pillow. With a deep sigh, she released the hold she'd had on her emotions and tears began to soak the fabric.

She was so tired.

She'd been pretending for so long.

Was her mother right? Was she not important enough for her father to visit? The last time her or Cecil had seen Philip was two years ago, when he was lugging his stuff out of the house and onto a truck. It was agony, she thought to herself.

She wanted her dad.

Not her mom.

Her dad.

Philp Franks was always the kinder, gentler parent between the two. Anytime Chelsea had any problems with school, her dad was there to listen and offer words of guidance. Laura, on the other hand, believed firmly in tough love. Unfortunately, that love became too rough over the years.

Suddenly, Chelsea heard something strange as she cried into her pillow. The sound made her stop sobbing, replacing sadness with fear. Hot air hit her ear, as someone was whispering sweet nothings to her. The comparison was apt, as she had heard a voice.

"He's never coming back."

The teenage girl jumped up, flailing off the bed. Once she hit the floor, she quickly pulled herself up, so she was kneeling. "Who said that?!"

A gust of wind slapped her in the face, so strong as to force her eyes closed. "You're never seeing him again."

The teenager scowled. "You're wrong, asshole." Her voice read brave, but her heart and brain were anything but. Why was she hearing voices now? She'd never done that before! Was she going crazy?

"You'll die before you get the chance to see him."

Her eyes widened, the air of bravery vanishing in an instant.

"You won't live to see twenty."

Breaking into a cold sweat, she swallowed hard. Was she

speaking with a demon of some kind? A god? Satan? Was the Devil trying to fuck with her? She'd never been a religious type, but perhaps then was the time to start praying?

Before she could have time to figure it out, the doorbell rang.

Her heart sank, her hand coming up to muffle her incoming screams.

"I'll get it," Cecil called out. Chelsea shook her head hard. No, she pleaded amongst herself. Don't let the Reaper get her, Big Brother. Please don't!

Anticipation gutted the purple-haired girl. She awaited the knocking on her door, the walk to her grave. "It's time to go," Laura would announce. "Good luck on the other side." Cecil would be upset, definitely. But there was nothing that could be done about it. Death waited for nobody.

However, Death appeared to make an exception this one time.

"You think you can just come to my house and apologize for what you did?!" Cecil shouted at their unexpected guest. "Get fucked, asshole!"

Chelsea crawled over to the door, lending an ear for the confrontation downstairs.

"Look Cecil," said the voice of an unknown guy. "I'm sorry we came to blows. I'm...I'm really sorry I hurt you. I'm sorry I attempted to ask your sister out on a date. Why can't we just let bygones be bygones?"

At the mention of her, Chelsea stood up and opened her door.

A boy wanted to ask her out. Was he hot? If so, she'd be more than happy to stick it to Cecil. Her nerves were still on fire, but perhaps some lovestruck eye candy would take her mind of things for just a little while.

The teenage girl hurried down the stairs, catching sight of a familiar face. Brunette, fit, and handsome, she recognized him as the new quarterback for the Seagulls; Sasha Balandin. She'd spoken to him a few times at school, but never paid him much mind. After all, he was a fucking dork, albeit an attractive dork.

"Hey Chelsea," Sasha said with a quick wave. "How much of the conversation, uh, did you hear?"

With a forced smile, she crossed her arms. "Enough."

He rubbed the back of his head. "So, uh, what do you say?"

Cecil grabbed him by his dirty football jersey. "Don't even think about it, asshole. You keep your filthy hands off my baby sister."

Chelsea stepped forward, still crossing her arms. "I can handle a guy, Cecil. Granted, of all people, I can't fathom how he made the football team."

"Well," Sasha answered with a grin. "I just so happen to be better at the game than your bro."

Cecil reared back to punch him in the face, but Chelsea grabbed his fist. "Stop it," she then looked at Sasha, forcing a smirk. "How does tomorrow night at seven sound?"

The quarterback's eyes grew three sizes, and his smile widened. "A-Absolutely! It's a date!"

She offered a genuine giggle, fighting through her traumatic experience with the paranormal. She never would've guessed she'd fall in love with the boy. At her ugliest, he'd stand by her. It was more than any man had done for her before.

The very end was coming soon.

In her final words, she'd tell Sasha she was sorry.

Chapter Eleven

130 Degrees

The explosion of projectile vomit splashed into the back of Barry's headrest. Chelsea's forehead was cold, her vision blurring. She had done what he asked, and she felt even closer to death than ever before. Not only had she sacrificed the last bit of fluid still in her body, but its foul taste was also soaking into her gums, making her more nauseous by the moment.

"*Bitch*," Barry uttered harshly. "You could've gotten puke in my hair!"

The streaked girl didn't listen to him. The momentum from her sickness was only picking up. She bent down and threw up all over the floorboard, soaking her feet. The mixed flavor of urine and bile made her wretch, producing more sick in the car. The smell of her own concoction of disgust made her empty stomach curdle.

She should've never listened to Barry.

His threats should've gone through one ear and out the other.

But she chose to take him seriously.

Now she was in much more agony.

And Barry could only smile.

"I'd rather not smell your putrid stomach gunk," he exited the car and rushed to the driver's side back door. Once Barry opened it, he yanked Chelsea by her hair. He pulled her out of the vehicle, dropping her onto her knees.

She didn't react at all to the pain.

She'd felt so much pain already; what was a little more?

"Show me how sick you are," Barry instructed. "All over the sand. I don't have all day."

She didn't want to give him what he wanted. He had proven to be a terrible person amongst the crew of college students; possibly the worst person she'd ever met. Laura Franks only wished she was as awful as Barry Waters.

And while the vomit and bile had ceased, that didn't stop Chelsea from hacking and gagging.

And Barry simply couldn't get enough of it.

***

Meanwhile, Sasha was trekking through the desert, desperate to find cacti that were ripe with water. There hadn't been any in the vicinity of the car, which had been why nobody had caved and done it already. Death Valley was already hot enough as it was; walking aimlessly through it was bound to kill them faster.

Sasha knew Chelsea was at the point of no return, but he that didn't mean he wanted to believe it. The woman had been his first real love. He wanted them to live and die together; there was no until death do them part. She was convinced the end was nigh, and maybe she was right.

No, Sasha told himself.

It couldn't end like this.

It just couldn't!

The Russian American dragged his tired feet through the desert. His joints ached and he hadn't even done a lot of walking. Though, perhaps that was why he was was in so much pain. The fact of the matter was that he *hadn't* done much walking in two days; he had been too afraid.

He regretted the decision more than anything. Had they walked around, they might've been able to find some valuable resources that would've prolonged their lives and made stranded life much easier. "Not true," Sasha muttered to himself. "There's fuck all out here."

"*Time wasted. Time wasted.*"

Hearing the husky voice harping at him in his ears, the brunette shook his head, giving his face a good slap. The whispers were still coming and going, though they were beginning to enjoy their vacation home. No amount of persuasion was making them want to leave.

"Empty-handed."

Sasha tugged at his hair. "Get out of my head."

"Here to stay."

He slapped his face once more. "Go away!"

Within a moment of arguing with the unwanted guests, Sasha spotted a saving grace off in the distance. It was a single baby cactus that seemed to have sprouted from the ground a least a week or two ago. It probably didn't even have so much as a drop of water within it. But he had to try; if not for himself, then for his woman.

Rikki was far gone into madness.

Barry had been possessed by the Devil.

They were doomed, but perhaps he could save himself and Chelsea, at the very least. If he had enough water to spare, he'd offer some to Rikki; Barry could rot for all he cared. People often said that situations like this often brought out the worst in others, but there's a fine line between madness and pure evil...or maybe there truly wasn't. Sasha hadn't any real way of knowing; he wasn't a psychologist by any means. He just wanted out of this fucking desert with as little death involved as possible.

So, when he spotted the baby cactus, Sasha hurried over. His legs were wobbly, trying and failing to support his weight.

"No," he muttered, trying his darndest to keep on his feet. "Not yet! I can still do this, dammit!"

But he couldn't, not really.

Within a couple feet from the source of water, Sasha tripped and fell face-first into the hot sand. His face was scorched, but like all his friends, the heat had become another part of their bodies. He had only the smallest reaction to the burn.

"Fuck."

Trying to get back up, his shaking hands pressed into the sand. "Ohh," he groaned, managing to pull himself up fair enough to look ahead. But he soon found himself shaking his head in disbelief. "No. *No*! You gotta be fucking kidding me! No!"

The baby cactus was gone.

Replaced with a noticeable heat wave.

Dejected, Sasha fell back into the sand, sobbing. "No, no, *no*! Why did this have to happen?!" The gravity of the situation was obvious by the second day, but maybe it hadn't really sunk in until that very moment. He realized the inevitable and his heart tore into two.

Chelsea was going to die, and there was nothing he could do about it.

Chapter Twelve

The Face of Evil

Sasha returned a little over an hour later, ultimately unsuccessful in his endeavor. His legs took a little while to recharge from his fall, but he was eventually able to walk his way back to the Chevy Malibu. If that baby cactus was going to follow him back, then he hoped its little roots would hurry the hell up. The brunette didn't like being tricked by people, let alone a place.

He felt used by the goddamn desert. For what? Wasn't his blood, sweat, tears, and soul more than enough to satisfy the great Hephaestus himself? Was nobody's suffering enough?

Once he arrived back at Barry's car, he could immediately see things hadn't got any better from when he left. Rikki continued to dance in the hot sun while wearing her birthday suit. The doors to the Chevy Malibu were wide open, the strong smell of puke permeating from it. "Guys?!" he called out, rushing to the other side of the vehicle.

From where he stood, he saw two horrifying sights. One was Chelsea, who was hunched over and gagging. The second was Barry, who hovered over her and smiled manically as she suffered. Sasha wasn't a very smart man, but he knew when something nefarious was going on.

"What the hell is going on here?!"

Chelsea didn't respond, instead just coughing up her lungs. She looked awful; hell, they all did. But there was something traumatizing about seeing one's one true love looking like they were moments away from falling over dead.

Barry, on the other hand, looked like he had embraced the sickness and learned to live as one with it. He also looked terrible, but he was in a different place than Chelsea. He wasn't on the ground. He wasn't emptying his stomach all over the sand. He was smiling, looking like he'd just woken up on Christmas morning.

"Hey, Buddy," Barry said with a small chuckle. "I'm positively swell. How about you?"

Sasha crouched down over Chelsea and rubbed her back. "Babe? *Babe*!"

The streaked girl coughed once more. "I-I don't have much t-time, Sasha."

"Don't say that," the brunette pleaded. "You'll get through this. You will."

Chelsea shook her head. "N-No, Sasha. I won't. And I've made my peace with it. You should too."

He shook his head slowly, biting his bottom lip. "Please, Chels. You have to keep fighting."

"I can't, she argued. "Even if I wanted to, Barry won't allow me to win. He's why my death will be even sooner than expected."

The blonde chuckled darkly. "You did that to yourself. You didn't have to do it."

Sasha quickly transitioned from comforting to seething. He stood up and grabbed Barry by his bare shoulders. "What did you do, Barry? What did you do?!"

Barry's eyes widened.

Sasha had broken the cardinal rule.

No touching.

"How *dare* you put your filthy hands on me," he growls, shoving him back. His next couple of words came out as harsh screams. "You have any idea who I am?! *What* I am?!"

"Yeah," Sasha shouted back. "You're Barry Waters! I don't know who *you* think you are, but I know you as you really are. You'll do well to remember who you are."

Barry shook his head. "No."

"You're Barry Waters," Sasha argued. "You're nineteen years old. You go to college in San Diego, California!"

"Stop it, Sasha," the deity warned.

"You're from Eureka. You're in love with Rikki Simmons. You're my best friend!"

"I said *stop it*!" Barry screamed.

"You're never going to be anyone else other than Barry Waters, dumbass," Sasha argued. "There's no changing who you are, so why try?!"

Having had enough, the blonde punched Sasha in the face, knocking him onto the ground beside Chelsea. The woman, once again, didn't react to the act of violence before her. Instead, she looked over at her man and sighed, forlorn.

"If you're going to kill me," Chelsea said. "Then make it fast. I'm tired of this. I'm tired of all of this. I just want to lay down long enough to die."

Sasha pulled himself up to his knees, rubbing the spot Barry had attacked. "No. You can't just quit now, Chelsea. I won't allow it!"

"Face it," Barry said, still glaring holes through the man who used to be his best friend. What simpler, more naive times those were. "You're only prolonging her suffering by insisting she fight. If you really loved her, you'd put her out of her misery."

The brunette seethed. "Fuck you."

Barry shrugged. "Okay. Then I'll kill her for you."

Before Sasha could properly react, the blonde reared back and uppercut kicked Chelsea's chin, sending her onto her back. "What the fuck, Barry?! Don't do this!"

Not listening to the Russian American, the blonde stood over the girl and started stomping out her neck as hard as he could. Sasha begged and pleaded, trying to push Barry off of her. But nothing was working. Chelsea spat up blood as she writhed in agony; the final screams she'll ever make.

"*Stop*!" Sasha screamed, finally managing to get the deity to stop attacking his woman. However, the damage had been done. Chelsea laid back, loudly coughing up blood. Tearing up, the brunette caressed the face of his lover.

"S-Sasha," she whimpered. "I'm so...sor..."

Before her words could come out, her breaths stopped. Her eyes laid open and vacant. Sasha shook his head slowly as he sobbed.

There was nothing Sasha could have done.

At least the suffering of Chelsea Franks had come to an end.

Chapter Thirteen

The End of Innocence

Two days had passed since Barry and his family had made it to Los Angeles. The day of the concert had come, and Kathleen and Gregory Waters were getting ready for the show within the hotel room. Barry, meanwhile, just sat quietly on his bed, staring at the carpeted floor. He wore his pajamas, but it was thirty minutes until noon.

The trip had gone well for the parents, but not the child.

No matter where he went, he always felt like something, or someone, was plotting to kidnap him; maybe even kill him. By that point, multiple instances of being grabbed by ethereal forces had occurred.

Being grabbed in the hotel lobby.

Being yanked around by an unknown entity within the bedroom, only mere feet away from his mother and father.

And any moment he wasn't paying attention was repaid with unkind generosity from this otherworldly being. Whether he was in the restroom, eating in a random Los Angeles restuarant, or riding around the city in his father's Honda HR-V, he would inevitably feel like he was being touched by something that wasn't there.

Sometimes it would just tug at his shirt. Other times, it would caress his face and shoulders, and there was even a point where he felt his hair being tugged. Young Barry didn't know what this being wanted, but he was horrified. Kathleen and Gregory didn't understand; they were too old to see why this had been so scary for the child.

"It's just a phase," his father muttered to his mother as they watched the boy stare at his own bare feet. "He's just overwhelmed by the new place. He'll be fine once we return home."

Kathleen sighed, gently pushing her hands under her son's armpits and lifting him up. "You think so, Greg?" Her husband pulled the sheets back and she laid the child down on his back. Barry just stared blankly at the ceiling as his parents talked about him as if he weren't around. "Los Angeles isn't too much different than Eureka. I wonder what has him so spooked?"

With a blink, the boy looked up at his mother with an expressionless face. "I'm not safe, Mom," he explained quietly. "I wanna go home."

Alas, his feeble attempt to warn his parents meant nothing. Kathleen just looked down at him with a smile that tried its hardest to be comforting, but it just wasn't. "You're completely safe in this room, honey," she murmured as she tucked him into bed. "No spookies are going to get you here. No sir."

"That's right, son," Gregory said calmly as he stuffed his arms through his denim jacket with metal band patches sewn on. "Nobody is going to nab you here. Nobody can get into the room without our card key, which is right here."

He patted his right pant pocket. This should've brought the boy some joy and comfort, but it only piqued his apprehension more. This thing didn't seem to need a card key to get to the child. Spirits rarely needed doors or walls to get to a target, so Barry knew his parents were just being stupid.

They needed to listen to him.

They needed to believe every word he said.

It wasn't a phase.

"Now just calm down," Kathleen said quietly as she planted a kiss on his forehead. "And get some sleep. We love you, kiddo."

Barry attempted to keep his eyes closed as his parents left the room to go to the Metallica show. His little feet bunched up under the comforter, his toes soaking in the heat like a sponge. His back laid straight on the memory foam mattress while his head sank a little on his fat pillow.

For any other kid, this would've been the life. No worries, no chores, not homework, no bossy parents. Just him and his cozy hotel room bed. Sleep would have him as a special guest at the nocturnal slumber party.

Unfortunately, Barry's company was demanded elsewhere.

As he felt the Sandman's presence loom over him, another entity vied for his focus instead. The creature screeched as it shoved the Sandman aside. Barry kept his eyes shut, daring not look into the forces that were beyond his understanding.

"Barry," came a harsh whisper that sounded like his father. But it couldn't have been him; he just left! There was no way he was going to return before the show happened, no way, Jose.

"Barry," the voice beckoned. "Barry Waters."

The boy squeezed his eyes shut and yanked his comforter over his blonde head of hair. "You're not real. You're not!"

The cold air outside the comforter clashed with the warmth underneath. Barry felt himself begin to feel disoriented. The only relief he could find from the temperature was his closed eyes, and even then, that couldn't last forever. "Please go away, the boy pleaded.

Within another moment, the voice spoke again. "Barry!"

Curiosity finally drove the boy over the edge and he opened his eyes. He would now get a look of his stalker. He would find the proof that he wasn't just some imaginative kid.

But there was no one there, at least not yet.

With one more blink, Barry screamed loudly.

Staring at him from underneath the comforter, the being

almost looked human...almost. His ghostly flesh somehow made the black eyes seem even darker. His red pupils dilated at the sight of fresh meat. The mouth was permanently agape, gnarly fangs poking out from the gums.

"Divinity!" the specter screamed, grabbing a hold of Barry. The child screamed, seizing like a fish out of water. The life force was seemingly being sucked out of his body. He wanted to get away, but the spirit was just too strong.

So, he seized.

And seized.

And seized.

The specter yanked at his limbs as if trying to feed. But he could never succeed, which made his eager attempts hurt even more. Young Barry felt his consciousness give way to the atmosphere. All that was left right at that moment was the tussle between him and this creature.

The tugging didn't stop for good hour. The seizing evolved from convulsions to limp unconsciousness. His parents returned, none the wiser of what had happened. And perhaps that was for the best.

Chapter Fourteen

Feast on the Sheep

Sasha hovered over the lifeless body of his lover. Her green eyes, once full of vigor and spunk, just stared blankly at the sky. Blood gently poured from her mouth, coating the sand around her neck. Chelsea Franks was no more, and it hurt the young man more than anything in the entire world.

"*Why*?" he asked quietly, shaking violently. "Why, Chelsea? *Why*?"

Barry popped a crick in his neck. He watched his "friend" grovel and mourn like a typical human would. If it were him, he'd be impressed by the deity's handiwork. Why let the bitch live when she was more useful dead?

And as he eyeballed the dead girl, Barry felt an indescribable force surge through his body like an electrical current. It was like a chill, but much more satisfying as it fired up into his spine. The feeling was incredible. He felt he could lift his car with one hand. There was only one thing he could determine about this feeling; it was truly powerful.

"My hypothesis was right," he murmured. "Killing you fuckers is my ticket to divinity." It was such an easy theory to concoct and he knew he was right all along. However, there was something satisfying about having the confirmation staring him directly in the eyes with that look of insatiable lust.

"Stop crying," Barry instructed, his voice booming. "We did what was necessary."

With a harrowing look, Sasha looked up at his former friend. "*We*? There's no we, only you. *You* killed her!"

With an ecstatic grin, Barry chuckled. "You let me," the blonde squatted onto the ground, dropping down to Sasha's level. "You wanna know why you couldn't save her, Sasha? Because I'm right. You know she was suffering. You agree that killing her was the right thing to do," he cocked an eyebrow. "So, I don't understand why you're so upset. Would you rather I didn't show her any mercy? I just did what you didn't have the balls to do yourself."

The brunette stared into the soulless eyes of his friend.

This wasn't Barry Waters.

He remembered Barry Waters, a man who would've given his left nut to help a friend. They had originally hit it off in U.S. History class. Barry was good with political history, but not so much history-history. The blonde could list off all the reasons J. Edgar Hoover was a bad president but couldn't remember the exact wording of General Grant's message to the South. So the men helped each other out; first study buddies, then friends.

Sasha fondly remember the ol' lug.

But he was gone.

He died the day the Chevy Malibu crashed in Death Valley.

This psychopath might've looked like him, but they were two different entities altogether.

"You're a fucking monster."

Barry shrugged. "Takes one to know one."

"I'm not the psycho killer here!" Sasha snapped, voice echoing throughout the desert.

The blonde watched the brunette for a moment. Sasha's bottom lip quivered and his whole upper half shook from anger and fear's lovechild. Barry contemplated killing him right then and there. Why take anymore detours on the road to divinity?

Because it was fun, he decided.

Why shouldn't he play with his food for a moment longer?

"You really don't think you're capable of taking another's life, Sasha? You really don't have it in you to kill for the sake of prolonging your own life?"

The Russian American shook his head. "What the actual fuck are you talking about? Killing Chelsea didn't prolong anything!"

Barry bit his bottom lip, stifling a laugh. "I'm closer to ascension, Sasha. Before long, my physical body will rot away and I'll manifest as something beyond human understanding."

Sasha growled loudly. "Enough of the god talk, dammit! You're not a god. You'll never be a god. You have absolutely nothing to gain by killing people!"

"Do I, though?" Barry asked, wagging his tongue within his mouth. "Look at yourself. You're actually convinced you'd never kill anyone to enhance your own power? The desert heat has obviously made you insane!"

Sasha bit his lip, trying not to point out the irony in his accusation.

"No matter," Barry continued. "I'm going to enlighten you on why I think you're so full of shit," he turned around and pointed at Rikki, who was still dancing aimlessly under the hot sun. "See her?"

Sasha nodded.

"Like what you see?"

The brunette glared at the man who used to be called "friend". "Where the hell is this going, Barry?"

The blonde chuckled once more. "Isn't it obvious? Or do I have to spell it out for you?"

Sasha looked over at the naked woman, trying to think of

a way to delay whatever horrible thing Barry had concocted in his sick head. "Spell it out for me, *Buddy*."

The deity flashed a toothy grin. "Very well," he held his hand up, holding two fingers. "There are two major things every man needs in order to function properly. You know what those are?"

Sasha glared at Barry.

"Food and sex," the blonde explained. "And as far as I'm concerned, you haven't had either in some time. Rikki is over there for the taking."

The Russian American's mouth dropped. "You fucking bastard. Are you...are you suggesting what I'm thinking you're suggesting?!"

"That I am," Barry answered with a nod. "Take that juicy pussy and then feast on her crispy flesh. It's the only way you're going to survive out here."

Sasha instantly stood up, screaming. "Are you nuts?! Rikki is our friend! You wanted to date her, remember?! Now you want us to..." he felt himself grow nauseous at the mere mention of Barry's twisted plan. "...eat her," he said with a gag. "And assault her. How fucking dare, you?"

Barry let out a wicked laugh, slapping his knees like an excitable chimpanzee. "You make an excellent point! Why should I let *you* have her?!" The blonde stood up, popping his knuckles as his laugher ceased. "You're right, Sasha. I will take Rikki. You can have Chelsea, though she won't move much for you."

Sasha's eyes widened. "I-I can't let you do that!" The brunette reared back to slug the blonde but was instantly downed with a kick in the nuts. "Ow, *fuck*!" he dropped to his knees, caressing his left thigh.

"Enjoy the show, Sasha," Barry murmured just before sprinting over to the dancing girl. Sasha wanted to get up and stop him. He wanted to save Rikki from a horrible fate. If he couldn't help Chelsea, he could at least help her.

But that's not what happened.

As Barry knocked Rikki to the ground, Sasha felt his vision begin to give out. In flashes he'd see what was going on. Flash one, Barry was on top of her. Flash two, he was pulling her arm up and biting into it. Flash three, he screams reverberated throughout the desert.

And all Sasha could do was watch.

Chapter Fifteen

The Third Night

Rikki Simmons died around sundown. Barry initially wanted to spare her so the men would have plenty to feast upon in the next coming days. But the woman had lost too much blood in just the one session. "I usually like rare meat," the blonde mused. "But now it looks like we'll have medium to medium well at this point, now that she's kicked the bucket."

Sasha couldn't bring himself to look Barry in the eye. The atrocities he had carried out during the day were far too heavy for the brunette to properly process. He had gone too far; as if killing Chelsea wasn't enough.

Rikki was always a good girl.

She didn't deserve her fate.

Sasha had to wonder if anyone else was going to die and, if so, just how awful was it going to be? He didn't think it was possible to top Rikki. Barry would really have to outdo himself if he were to try upping the ante with Sasha's death.

Don't say that, Sasha thought to himself. He wasn't going to die. If anything, Barry would be the one to die. Not only had he gone completely insane, he also ate human flesh. Not that Rikki was a disgusting person, but her entire body was coated in sweat. So much bacteria lives in the human body. Surely the build-up would be enough to kill the beast of a man.

If it wasn't enough, then Sasha didn't know what else to do. Killing Barry would've been a mercy at that point, but then he'd be no better than him. Unlike the blonde, Sasha took no solace in causing harm to others. Had his mind gone? Just a little. But he was still able to be saved; Barry was not.

Rather than killing him, what better fate was there than to leave him to die in Death Valley? He wanted to be a god so badly, let him become a god of one. Sasha wanted no part of his worship, and he was going to find a way to escape this hell. He'd have a lot of explaining to do.

Where was everyone?

Did they ever make it to Vegas?

Why was Sasha in desperate need of medical treatment?

The psychiatric care he'd need was also on the forefront of his mind. The hallucinations were ongoing and now he witnessed not one, but two very brutal murders committed by his best friend. He had no one left to trust. If he was going to survive, he'd need a plan.

But before he could properly plot out his escape, he had something he needed to do.

It was the most morally apt thing to do.

Barry had left the girls lying on the sand, dead without even a proper burial. He just left them out to rot like roadkill. Sasha was sure Barry would come to regret that choice later when the sun came back out. But knowing the sick bastard that was accompanying him, he'd probably relish in taking seconds from Rikki; possibly firsts from Chelsea.

It was shameful, Sasha thought to himself.

Beyond disrespectful.

It was salt in the wound.

"They're people," the brunette growled at the blonde, who was stargazing a little way off from the Chevy Malibu. "They're *people*, dammit! And you're just leaving them out here like cannon fodder!"

Barry said nothing; the one-time Sasha didn't want him to keep quiet.

"Say something!" the brunette demanded. "Tell me why you're right to do all of this!"

The blonde stayed silent.

"*Answer me!*"

The "deity" didn't budge, nor utter a single peep. Sasha wasn't sure what was scarier; Barry acknowledging his exis-tence or him ignoring him. Either way, the Russian American knew what he needed to do, and he was going to do it regardless of what Barry said or did.

So, while the blonde stared up at the night sky, Sasha took advantage and wandered away from the scene of the crime. He needed a good spot to bury the girls. Would Barry even notice if their bodies were gone? There was no telling; he might've been under the impression that the spirits whisked them away as to not offend his Holiness with the foul stench of death.

Granted, Barry smelled far worse than Chelsea and Rikki combined, even with the open wounds. He already stunk of fermented sweat, but now the smell of blood and exposed muscle tissue reeked off of him. Sasha was thankful to be away from the "deity" for more reasons than one, needless to say.

As Sasha stepped away, he fought through the unsteadiness of his legs so he could trek through the cool desert.

***

He didn't look his way, but Barry already knew where Sasha was going. The brunette was as easy to read as a graphic novel. Wandering off in the middle of the night? Giving the blonde an unnecessary attitude about the two dead bitches by the car?

Sasha was looking to escape Death Valley.

The desert had grown old for the ol' lug.

Or perhaps he was scared shitless of the deity before him? He thought Barry was going to target him next. Well, he was absolutely right about that. If Barry Waters wanted to reach true godhood, he had to take out the competition. It was obvious that the four students were skillfully chosen for some kind of divine game. Let them live in squalor until the realize their sheer power. Whoever won would taste the lips of immortality, not for the body, but the soul.

Two were down, only one to go. The Russian American was still going, albeit not strongly at all. He had bad legs, poor balance, and was hearing things that scared him. Barry smiled. He was better than him. He learned to love the voices, not fear them.

Nevertheless, it was concerning that nothing was taking Sasha down. No hunger, no heat, no water, no cleanliness of the mind...nothing to his name, and yet he still persevered! Sasha Balandin should've died a long time ago!

Barry scowled at the sky. The brunette didn't say it out loud, but his intentions were as obvious as black clouds forecasting a grisly thunderstorm. Sasha aimed to steal the blonde's well-deserved throne. Sure, he talked big talk in which he defied divinity, but all those things weren't said because they were true.

It was said because the Russian American was jealous of him.

Sasha wanted so badly to be a god that he was willing to try and manipulate Barry into giving up his pilgrimage to the other side. That wasn't going to happen, he thought to himself. The brunette wasn't nearly smart enough to convince Barry of anything. "What an insult to my intelligence," he murmured to nobody. "And to his own."

The deity slowly blinked as he stared up into space. To think all that was holding him back from flying up into those very stars was the heartbeat of one man. It was such a silly little stipulation. Barry was obviously being tested by neighboring deities. Yahweh, Shiva, Isis, Horus, Ra, whoever might've been dwelling over this desert, watched him and judged accordingly.

Barry was positive that the gods above were pleased with his handiwork thus far. He'd taken helpless prisoners like the vengeful, fun-loving deity he knew himself to be. They needed someone with such chaotic energy to control the desert. Nobody else but him could do it. Barry had adapted to the hellscape and no longer felt like he was at the mercy of a cruel, unforgiving set of circumstances.

If that wasn't enough to warrant divinity, then he didn't know what was.

Did the desert tear him to shreds? Of course it did. However, with pain comes growth. Sasha wouldn't get to experience that miracle of life, not on Barry's watch. If the two skanks couldn't experience it, what made the brunette think he could?

The women served their purpose.

Chelsea served as a guinea pig for the almighty deity's plan for godhood.

Rikki, though?

She was a fine piece of meat.

Barry felt like a new man now that he had some sustenance in his stomach. The red-head's blood tasted like aluminum foil and her skin was flavorless save for the salt of her sweat, but all that mattered to Barry was that he wasn't hungry anymore. His formerly weakened muscles regained some strength.

And he hadn't even touched the magnificent way Miss Rikki Simmons had helped him get his rocks off. She was tighter than a lock, screaming in pleasure as his semen poured from out of her body. Barry might've been disgusted by her, but the one thing that didn't change from his previous life was that he found her utterly beautiful. Even in her deceased state, he found her tantalizing to look upon.

But that was neither here nor there.

Barry's focus needed to be on Sasha, not some bimbo from his past.

The brunette was a fool for not listening to him. Not that it mattered anymore, of course. Sasha was going to die in a day's time. For that moment, however, Barry needed some sleep. Even deities slumbered.

The plan was simple.

Once the morning hit, Sasha Balandin would be no more.

Barry would ascend to the heavens, where he rightfully belonged.

The blonde turned the key on Sasha's doomsday clock.

It ticked fast.

***

The sand was naturally cold at night, Sasha noticed. It was a stark contrast to how it felt during the daytime. If it weren't for the corns and callouses in his feet, he would've taken his shoes off and soaked his toes into the cool sand. But alas, there was simply too much agony in the lower half of his body.

It would've been a miracle if he could carry Chelsea and Rikki to their graves without falling over. The first step was easy; find an ideal place to start digging. Sasha managed to find a spot in the ground that was significantly cooler than the surrounding sand. He didn't know if the daytime heat would've made the resting place a respectless location to bury the women.

What if the sun shined directly on top of them, making them rot even faster and causing their dead smell to permeate the air far enough to reach the car? That simply wouldn't do, but what other choice did Sasha have? He needed to ditch the bodies fast, lest Barry decide to inflict further damage to the corpses.

That meant Chelsea and Rikki would have to share a grave. He figured Chelsea wouldn't have minded; her and Rikki were good friends. "This spot will do," he whispered to himself. "If only I had a shovel."

The temptation to check the trunk of Barry's car was strong, but there were a number of factors working against him. For one, Barry would be suspicious and try to stop him from bury- ing the girls. For two, if there had been a shovel in the trunk, they would've seen it during the first two days of their excur- sion. For three, Sasha wasn't strong enough to shovel sand, not at the present moment.

"Fuck it," he murmured, crouching down. Like a dog, Sasha began pawing at the sand in the attempt to dig a hole. Was this a stupid idea? Absolutely. Was it all he could muster the strength to do? Definitely.

He was sure it would be an all-night affair and he'd potentially have to deal with Barry's wrath before he could get the chance to bury Chelsea and Rikki. "Don't think that," he muttered aloud. "I will get this done in time. I swear it."

Chapter Sixteen

In Loving Memory

The first couple of sweeps weren't too terrible for the Russian American. In the hopes of expediting the process, he scooped large piles of sand at a time. He didn't need the hole to be too deep; just deep enough to sufficiently hold two small-framed feminine bodies. So long as there wasn't a lot of wind during the night, Sasha didn't have much of a worry of sand blowing off the bodies.

With that being said, he still wanted to ensure the grave was deep enough. "What the hell is wrong with me?" Sasha wondered aloud. "I'm burying my woman and her friend. I should be killing their murderer," the man bit the inside of his lips, trying to hold back an emotional meltdown. "I-Instead, I'm here wondering how deep to dig a fucking hole."

A sob broke out of the brunette, stopping him mid-scoop. He rested on his palms and cried. No tears came out, as his body's fluids were also walking on a thin tightrope. If he became anymore dehydrated, then he was sure he'd be done in. Barry would get exactly what he wanted.

"*D-Dammit!*" he shouted. "This is fucked up. Fucking *bull-shit!*" He pounded his fists into the ground, whimpering loudly. "Fuck!"

Pull yourself together, he told himself. He had a task to do, and he was on quite the time crunch. If he wanted to save the dignity of Barry's victims, he had to bury them before sunrise. "Right," he grunted, continuing his frantic dig.

Like a cat sharpening its claws, the man stretched his torso just enough to increase the size of the hole. Rikki was a little shorter than Chelsea, but both women were in the five-foot-something range. So, the grave didn't have to be tall by any stretch of the imagination, at least not tall enough to support a grown man.

After a good hour or so of the obsessive scooping of sand, Sasha had eventually dug a satisfyingly deep hole. "Good work, Sash," he told himself. "Now to hurry and grab the girls."

Realistically, Sasha would have to bring the women to the open grave one at a time, as his legs still felt like jelly. But who would he bring first? It shouldn't have been a matter worth debating, so long as both were safe from any further tyranny from Barry. But the brunette couldn't help but mull over the pros and cons.

Rikki was the worst off out of the two. Her open wounds made her body smell atrocious, her blood still fresh as she laid on her back on the cold desert floor. Sasha felt that he needed to do her a mercy and bury her first.

But, on the other hand, Chelsea would've been less messy

to place into the grave. Her blood had dried under the Death Valley sun. She still stunk, but the smell was so much more tolerable. But Sasha couldn't help but feel the emotional turmoil of burying his lover would take its toll on him. He never thought he'd ever have to bury Chelsea Franks, but there he was, and it hurt so much.

What was it going to be?

The dead girlfriend, or the partially devoured friend?

...

It would be Rikki first.

He couldn't handle the sensation of burying Chelsea just yet.

"Let's do this," he muttered as he stood up. Quite literally dragging his feet, Sasha hobbled back over to the crashed car. Upon arrival, he noticed Barry had been laying down still. However, his posture suggested great comfort; he was asleep.

The Russian American sighed with relief. Not looking to shake the tree, Sasha snuck over to the deceased Rikki Simmons. Flies had begun to fly over her, attracted to the smell of her open wounds, which were on her arms and neck. What a disgrace, Sasha thought to himself. Barry couldn't possibly live with the disgusting shame now resting within his stomach.

If he could, then he was truly unworthy of being saved.

"Let's go, Rikki," he whispered as he attempted to lift her up into a fireman carry. He lasted about two minutes before his legs gave out. "Ah!" he held onto the woman as he fell backwards. Her body laid on top of his, blood pouring onto his bare chest.

Sasha wanted to scream, but he refrained by covering his mouth with his hand. He shook with fear as he waited a moment to see if Barry would stir from his slumber. When he did not, Sasha quickly pushed the red head off of him. "Sorry, Rikki," he whispered as he slowly got onto his knees.

There was no way he was going to be able to carry her, he realized. He had no choice but to drag her through the sand. Sasha felt bad about doing her dirty like that, but it was what it was. "Let's do this." he murmured. "Take two."

Sasha grabbed Rikki's ankles and stood up. Taking his time, he slowly dragged the woman to her grave. The walk luckily wasn't too far; just far enough to be out of sight from Barry Waters. He shivered at what he'd have to do next.

He couldn't carry her and gently lower her into the hole.

He'd have to drop her from above.

With a defeated sigh, Sasha dragged his feet to the grave and swung his torso. Letting go of the woman, she fell into the grave. Her neck landed into a position that looked as though it had been snapped. If she wasn't dead before, she certainly was then.

"I'm so sorry," Sasha whispered just before walking back to the car. Now it was Chelsea's turn. Like Rikki, he'd have to drag his lover through the sand and, also like Rikki, he'd feel like shit for doing so.

Still relishing in the dark sky, Sasha made it back to the Chevy Malibu. Stepping around to the driver's side, he laid his eyes upon Chelsea Franks. She looked peaceful in a fucked-up sort of way. Nothing changed the fact that she was dead, but she wasn't suffering anymore.

That was one thing Barry was right about.

"Chelsea..." He crouched down and grabbed onto her ankles. Standing up, he turned around and dragged her through the desert. His heart was broken into a million pieces. All was said and done, but that didn't erase the regrets swirling around Sasha's head.

He was truly sorry.

But that wasn't enough this time.

Chapter Seventeen

A Little Piece of Heaven

Chelsea Franks was dropped onto Rikki deep within the grave. Sasha watched her body fall, closing his eyes upon her landing. "Goodbye, my love," he murmured with great melancholy. "See you on the other side." He covered his mouth with his left palm, trying his best to not have another meltdown.

The man shook.

Of course, it seemed like he was always shaking these days.

Sasha was perpetually afraid. Barry scared the living shit out of him; possibly more than being stuck in Death Valley with no clear way out. At least there was the smallest possibility that he'd find some help in the desert. The probability of it was scant, but it was there.

Staying with Barry, on the other hand, offered no chance of survival. He'd already killed twice before; what was stopping him from doing it a third time? Was it possible that the tiniest sliver of platonic affection still existed within the blonde? Or was he simply buying time?

For what, Sasha wasn't certain.

And that scared him even more.

Just how long was Barry going to wait? Until Sasha's suffering was no longer entertaining? The brunette dared not ponder for too long on the subject. All that would come from that was wasted time. Sasha hadn't a second to spare if he was going to live through this.

But God, was it hard.

He could've prevented her death.

He could've even prevented Rikki's.

"No," he said aloud, opening his eyes. "Nothing could've stopped this from happening..." Sasha looked up at the night sky, not a cloud in sight. "...right?"

A forlorn sigh escaped the brunette. "Fuck me. It's all lies; every little bit of it." Another sorrowful sob popped out of him. If only his football team were there to watch him. They'd rag on him so hard for being a crybaby. That humiliation would go on until Cecil Franks arrived.

How the hell was he going to tell him that his sister was dead? Cecil already wanted an excuse to kick Sasha's ass; this was going the extra mile. "Chelsea," the man whimpered. "Don't make me bury you. Don't make me say goodbye forever."

And then suddenly, much to the disbelief of the young man, Chelsea's head twisted around, her neck cracking loudly. She opened her eyes, revealing milky white irises and glossy pupils. She looked up at her man. "*Sasha.*"

Jaw dropped; the young man gasped. "N-No!" He backed away from the hole, but the woman wasn't done with the conversation yet.

"*Sasha!*" In an instant, Chelsea pushed herself up, snapping her head back to its proper position. With the reflexes of a cat, the dead girl rapidly climbed up the sandy grave, not foundering in the slightest at the loose sand. Sasha tried to back away quickly, but his legs gave out again and he fell over onto his ass.

The awakened corpse emerged from the hole, getting onto her feet so fast that Sasha could swear she stopped time in its tracks. The brunette frantically crept backwards as her neck snapped loudly so she could stare him down.

Sasha had seen plenty of horror movies in his short time on the planet Earth. He'd seen films about ghosts, demons, zombies, slasher villains, and even inanimate objects. The brunette wasn't sure if what he was seeing was a ghost, demon, zombie, or all of the above. Regardless of what she was, Sasha felt sick to his stomach looking at her.

In most horror movies, the villain was a fun-loving psychopath who took the lives of their victims with a smile on their face. They'd laugh, joke, and kill with their sick but jovial attitude. Even their twisted anecdotes could bring a nervous grin over the face of scared movie-goers.

Chelsea was no such being.

No laughing eruption.

No jokes.

No funny stories.

Miss Franks wasn't a fun-loving entity; she was far from it.

"*Sasha!*" she screamed as she bolted for his downed body. The man just couldn't back away fast enough. Before he knew it, his deceased lover was on top of him, her hands around his neck. "*Why, Sasha?!*" she screeched. "*Why didn't you save me?!*"

The brunette gasped for air. "Y-You were d-dying! W-What else could I do?!"

Chelsea reared back and screamed loudly in his face, her foul breath testing his gag reflex. "*Bullshit! Bullshit, Sasha!*" She squeezed on his neck. "*You're stronger than him! You could've taken him!*" Her face inched closer to his. "*Some god you turned out to be!*"

Still gasping for air, Sasha worked to try prying her cold hands off of his neck. "W-What do you mean by that?!"

"*You really don't know?!*" she screamed, finally letting go of him. "*You're a divine god, Sasha! I thought it was more than obvious! How else would you still be alive?!*"

Breathing fast and hard, Sasha shook his head. "I-I don't

believe you, Spirit. I won't fall into the same rabbit hole as Barry did."

Chelsea's neck snapped again as she quickly looked back at the car. "*His Heaven is a lie,*" she said calmly. "*Yours was told in the prophecy.*"

His breath steadying a little, Sasha raised his eyebrows. "Prophecy? What prophecy?"

"*Um,* the *prophecy!*" she screeched. "*The only one that matters! Where good vanquishes evil! What do you say? You wanna save me and Rikki and claim your rightful spot in the sky?*"

Sasha cocked an eyebrow. "Are you saying that if I kill Barry, I'll be the only true God?"

"*That's exactly what I'm saying,*" the corpse bellowed. "*Now stop fucking around and get to work!*"

Sasha blinked slowly. It was all too much for him to process properly. Him, a god? They chose *him* to rule as King of the Desert? They chose him to revive the soul of his lover and her friend. They needed him to kill off his biggest adversary for the sake of humanity.

"I can save you, Chelsea?" Sasha asked, reeling from the discovery. "I can turn back time and ensure you never perish?"

Staring down at him with her milky while eyes, she leaned down and planted a chaste kiss on his lips before climbing off of his body. The man bent upwards to see her falling back into her grave with Rikki.

So, it was settled, then.

Sasha would earn his divinity through justice and not malice.

Barry Waters would die.

And not a moment too soon.

Chapter Eighteen

Cat and Cat

It was around dawn when Barry rose from his slumber. For the first time since he'd been stuck in Death Valley, he managed to get a good night's sleep; possibly the best night's sleep he'd ever had. His skin barely hurt anymore; he either had gotten used to the pain, or the nerves in his flesh were all dead. His muscles, however, ached still.

But that didn't really matter to the god.

Mere mortal problems would soon be a burden of the past.

The blonde sat up and stretched his arms. He released a roaring yawn, squeezing his eyes closes shut. Maybe it was just his ears, but Barry felt his roar was heard all over the desert. The tiniest scorpion to the largest snake heard their lord's call and awakened with the desert sun. What they would do during their hours of sunlight was simple; they'd do what they'd always done; serve their king.

Yes, it was obvious that Barry was always the one. Rather than fear the touch of another, he could embrace the duty to touch others; spiritually and physically speaking. It was a lesson Barry needed to learn the hard way, as his boyhood was filled with foolish naivety. Why understand scary things when you could just run from them? What a cowardly stance to take!

It was only a shame that it took the shedding of his own skin for Barry to finally realize that he never had anything to fear at all. Then again, he supposed that anyone could become a god if they just learned to stop fretting and love the suffering. Barry Waters was thankful that he was the one to realize that first; lest he be forced to split his portion of the divinity pie. Gone were the days of generosity! When this god was hungry, he demanded to be fed!

Speaking of food, the deity opened his eyes and looked around the totaled vehicle. Not only had Sasha wandered off, but the ladies had also grown invisible tendrils that lifted them off the ground. Barry smirked. "Interesting, Balandin. Taking meat all for yourself, I see."

The blonde sat up, setting his hands into his lap. "He won't make it far. The valley is too wide and barren. He'd die within a matter of hours," Barry popped a cricked in his neck. "He'll come crawling back soon. I've still won."

***

As the false god had his back turned, Sasha stared from off in the distance. All that stood between the defiler and himself was heat waves and deepening mounds of sands. His legs ached still, but he was more than capable of kicking this little boy's ass.

And so, he charged at a slow, but stout pace. Pushing through the pain in his calves, Sasha Balandin channeled the athlete he once was in high school. The QB for the Seagulls, baby. That's who he started off as; he would end as the rightful protector of this valley.

"*Barry*!" he shrieked through the agony. "Face me!"

The blonde stood up, quickly turning to face his adversary.

He smiled.

***

So, the pussycat sought the feral lion.

The lowly beast wanted the fish so badly that he was willing to make the better sacrifice.

And Barry couldn't have been happier than to oblige.

"The balls on you," the blonde called out calmly. "Thinking you can waltz over here and take what's mine. You can barely walk!"

Sasha bit his lip as he hurried over, wishing he had a rock to chuck at his fat head. "Oh yeah?" the brunette called out. "At least my divinity is real. I'm not some kind of false prophet!"

Barry's eyebrows rose up into his forehead. "Interesting claim!" Did your dead hoe and her prudish bitch of a friend tell you that?"

At that that moment, Sasha took his fighting stance. Much like his particularly roughneck means of kicking ass, it needed to be a finely tuned wind instrument in a sea of drums. Protect the powerless like the hero Sasha Balandin was told he was.

He muttered a quiet "Thank you" to a girl who wasn't there anymore...for now.

Sasha would bring Chelsea and Rikki back.

Barry being missing would just be another listless tragedy that the brunette would have on his mind as he ruled over the desert. Existence was pain that deities like him needed to be used to if they wanted to protect pilgrims on their trek through Death Valley. It was necessary sacrifice.

And once Sasha approached the blonde, he greeted him with a painful headbutt into his forehead. Barry recoiled back with a hiss. "*Bastard*!" Taking advantage of his enemy's stunned state of being, Sasha threw himself on top of the false god's body, stabbing his face repeatedly with his knuckles. His legs might've had it, but his arms still had it in them.

Beggars couldn't be choosers, after all.

So long as he could best the blonde man, nothing else mattered to Sasha.

And so, the brunette pummeled Barry hard, bloodying up his nose and mouth. "This is for the girls, you sick fuck," Sasha exclaimed aloud. "How do you sleep at night, anyway?!"

Before Sasha could land his abteenth blow, Barry caught his

fist and tossed him aside. With a thud, the blonde switched positions with the brunette. "Pretty well, truth be told!"

And then it was Barry's turn to inflict damage, and he was must less kind to the man formerly known as his friend. Digging his fingernails into Sasha's face, he pulled down on the flesh. The brunette's skin ripped little by little, a byproduct of prolonged heat exposure.

Sasha refused to give him what he wanted, so he kept his mouth shut rather than screamed Bloody Mary. If he was going to win, he would have to outlast the psychopath above him. "I will rip your fucking face off," Barry growled, tightening his grip on the dry skin of Sasha Balandin.

Granted, the brunette's legs hurt a bit more than his face did. So much so that he groaned in agony whenever Barry put all his weight into his knees, pressing into the bones and muscles of Sasha's thighs. "Get off me!"

"Oh?" Barry taunted with a grin. "You want me to stop? Need I remind you that you started this? I'm simply finishing it."

"You killed them!" Sasha bellowed, forcing his legs upwards, allowing him to flip Barry over back onto his back. The brunette climbed back on top of him, wrapping his hands around his neck. "As the ruler of this new world, I will do away with people like you once and for all!"

Sasha squeezed tightly.

Barry chortled.

Luckily for the real God, pain wasn't going to get in the

way of ascension. Barry quickly reached down and grabbed at Sasha's knees, giving them a tight squeeze. The brunette howled in pain but managed to persevere in choking out his adversary.

Suddenly, the sky above went dark. Both men stopped fighting, Sasha falling off of Barry and landing beside him. The breathed loudly, staring up at the stars.

"We were...we were really...for that long?"

Barry nodded. "Looks like it. And if time flew for us both, I'd say time is meaningless because we're both divine."

A harsh cough exploded from out of Sasha. "You're wrong; there's no we. Only I."

"Be it as it may," Barry argued. "We will need to show the universe some equal attention. For instance, what is something you notice about the sky tonight?"

Sasha stared closely, not noticing anything yet.

Once it came into his mind, Sasha couldn't hold back his incoming shriek upon seeing the literal writing in the wall.

Chapter Nineteen

Four

"Stop screaming," Barry commanded. "For a supposed deity, you certainly are a wuss."

Sasha shook his head, jaw dropped. "What does this even mean?!" His breath was short and frantic, for he saw a particular image in the sky. All of the stars had entered a new formation. Instead of being scattered out, they grouped together in very distinctly shaped clusters, straight lines, like tally marks.

There were four of them.

Four clusters.

Four people.

Four souls.

Some pieces began to fit, but Sasha wasn't sure what the puzzle was supposed to present. Were the four college students fated to die in this desert? Why? What spiritual significance did they have that required their blood be spilled on the sand of Death Valley?

"I don't understand, Barry. I really don't!"

The blonde sighed. "If you'd give the universe time to explain, maybe you'll figure it out. Seriously, how can you expect to rule over anything with that attitude?"

"Says the guy who killed my girlfriend and ate the girl he wanted to date," Sasha retorted bitterly.

Barry snorted. "Divinity comes with sacrifices, asshole. They served their holy purpose. Perhaps you'd know that if you'd..."

A gentle hum off in the distance distracted Barry from finishing the point he was making. "You hear that?" he asked quietly.

Sasha nodded. "For once, yes. I do hear it."

It was quiet but audible enough to touch the brunette's eardrums. It made Sasha think about a Buddhist temple, full of meditating monks. No rush, no indignation. Just steady as she goes. It was calming to listen to, albeit hauntingly so.

"They're chanting for me," Barry determined. "My followers from all over the world."

Sasha listened closely, as he gave Barry's claim pause. It certainly sounded like they were saying something, but it didn't say his name or any name. In fact, it didn't even sound like English. If anything, it sounded like a sacred mantra, chanted entirely in Chinese.

"I'm not so sure, man," Sasha murmured. "I don't understand anything they're saying."

Barry gritted his teeth. "It's because you're a mere peon. You aren't meant to understand what they're saying. Only gods can make it out. That's me."

The brunette rolled his eyes, as he let the mantra enter one ear and exit the next. With time, however, the mantra began to sound smoother. If Sasha didn't know any better, he'd say that he was starting to understand them. Either that, or they wanted him to understand what they were chanting.

For a quick moment, the gentle chanting began to sound crackly and distorted. It reminded Sasha of the faceless adults from the *Peanuts* cartoons. Within a minute, the words began to familiarize themselves with the brunette.

"*Bow...bow...bou...*"

Barry must've thought they were saying this name because it started with a "B". But Sasha wasn't so sure that they were hearing the same thing. Besides, he refused to give that fucker any clearance. He didn't deserve to be revered by any spiritual get-together.

"Barry," the blonde murmured to himself. "Barry, Barry..."

Sasha had no doubt that Barry was hearing his name; what he doubted, really, was the blonde's ears. Nothing had made sense ever since they wrecked in the desert. Even the wreck itself made no sense.

The brunette listened closer. "*Bou...nd. Bound.*"

Sasha's eyes widened. "Bound?" he whispered to himself. "What's bound, and by what?" Was he bound by his humanity; only free once Barry was out if the picture? Were Rikki and Chelsea's lives bound by the curse which lied within this special part of Death Valley?

Sasha needed to hear more.

He desperately needed to know what was going on.

"Barry, Barry, Barry..."

The blonde's voice grew louder, making the brunette strain to hear any developments in the chanting. But he persevered; he had to.

"*Bound...by. Bound by...*"

"Barry! Barry! Bar--"

"Will you shut up, man?" Sasha snapped. "I'm trying to listen. I'm close to figuring out what they're really saying."

The blonde scoffed. "I'm telling you what they're saying."

Sasha listened further.

"*Bound by...bound by...*"

"Barry...Barry..."

"Bound by...bound by...fo...ur. Bound by four..."

"Barry...Barry...Barry..."

Sasha growled. "Seriously man, stop it. They are not calling for you. I hear what they are really saying."

"Yeah?" Barry said mockingly. "Well then, *God*. What are they saying if not my name?"

Sasha closed his eyes.

"Bound by four...tied to...die."

Barry sat up, turned to look at his former friend. "Yeah, that's not what I'm hearing at all," with his soulless eyes, an evil smirk swept across his face. "They're chanting for me. Not for us, Sasha. Not for Chelsea, and not for Rikki. *Me*."

The Russian American shook his head. "No, that's not right. They aren't calling for you at all."

In a short flash, Barry bent over and pressed his hand into Sasha's Adam's apple hard. His icy cold eyes froze the brunette's soul. "Are you deaf? How can you you not hear it?! How can you not hear the real message?!"

"What message even is that?" Sasha barked. "That you're awesome?!"

Barry pressed harder into Sasha's throat, growling loudly. "*Yes*! I'm a fucking God, you cock-sucking pissant. You'll do well to remember that."

"Listen to me, you fucking bastard!" Sasha screamed. "You aren't a god! You'll never be a god! They are not chanting you name!"

Frazzled by the apparent blasphemy, Barry let go of Sasha's throat and quickly stood up. "What does "Bound by four, tied to die" even mean?"

Sasha frowned. "It's it obvious? We were never meant to live in this desert. We're all doomed to die," the brunette then sat up. "But since I'm the only one hearing this, that tells me I was correct; I'm the real god here, not you."

Barry snorted. "Bullshit."

"Why can't you just open your eyes and *believe me,* man?" Sasha asked. "Is it because you're jealous? I'm a benevolent god, though I won't offer you much mercy for all the things you've done. But I may let you go, start a new life away from everyone and everything."

"You're wrong!" Barry insisted. "You speak heresy!"

Now it was Sasha's turn to step up to his feet. "Is it? It sounds like the absolute truth. Why else would I hear the real message and you can't?"

The blonde's eyes widened. "Liar!"

The two men got into each other's faces, noses inches away from each other.

"You're a false god, Barry," Sasha said. "You aren't divine; just a narcissistic pretender!"

And just like that, the fist fight continued. Barry launched a punch at Sasha's face, but the brunette caught his fist. In retailiation, Sasha slugged the blonde in the jaw. Bucking back, Barry then lunged forward and grabbed onto his former friend.

Barry landed a couple of gut punches before shoving him onto the ground. Sasha landed hard, but not so much that he couldn't sit up and scoot back. Unfortunately, due to the brunette's legs, the blonde managed to stand over him and squat. He grabbed a fistful of Sasha's hair and began pummeling his face.

Both men soon matched with the blood on their faces. In the attempt to relieve himself of the afflicted pain, Sasha threw his hands up and wrapped them around Barry's neck. The blonde, not looking to be done in, did the same thing to the brunette.

The two men proceeded to strangle each other.

They squeezed with all of their might, not relenting for even a second.

Sasha's vision attempted to give out, Barry's face blurring before him. But that was okay because the blonde was in the same predicament. The false god's face puffed up as he gasped for air. For a moment, it seemed as though Sasha was going to die soon.

"You're...you," Barry gasped. "...you a-are the...fourth caller in the queue."

Thrown off by the sudden statement, Sasha let go of his neck. Luckily, Barry also let go. In fact, he stood up and began to stagger away from the brunette. "You are the fourth caller in the queue." He tugged at tufted of his own hair. "You are the fourth caller in the fucking queue, Sasha! *You are*! *Your call is very important to us*!"

With an agonizing scream, Barry looked over at Sasha with big eyes. "*Your call is very important to us, Sasha*!"

The brunette shook his head. "What are you even talking about, man?"

Without even answering, Barry sprinted off into the desert.

"Barry?!" Sasha called out, now sitting up. "This isn't over yet, asshole! I'm going to rip that fat skull out of your head!"

Chapter Twenty

The Fallen Hero

"Your call is very important to us."

"Your call is very important to us."

"You are the fourth caller in the queue."

Barry's head was bloated, fat with thoughts racing at one hundred miles per hour. Why were these thoughts entering his head? Was Sasha right? Was Barry a false god? What was with this latest development in the grand scheme of things?

The significance of the number four began to weigh heavily on the would-be deity. Evidence pointed in two different directions: one at his own divinity, and one at the inevitability of death. He didn't want to die in this desert. He had so much he wanted to do in life first.

Graduate college.

Get married.

See the world!

But there were the damn voices, too! Weren't they steering him in the right direction? The visions before his very eyes! They wouldn't have possibly been wrong!

Right?

Could he no longer trust his own eyes? Sure, maybe ascension had its own funny way of interpreting fate. Ethereal nature tended to be extremely vague in movies and TV shows, after all. Riddles and symbols were often the way their messages were given and perhaps Barry just needed to get a grip and get with the program.

But why hadn't Sasha cracked yet? Rikki and Chelsea didn't last long at all, for they were simply too weak to handle the desert. But he and Sasha had lasted this long. How? Sasha hadn't the wherewithal to be a god! Only Barry had the stomach to sacrifice others for the sake of prophecy; he'd done it twice already!

"Fourth caller," he murmured to himself. "Fourth caller, fourth caller..." he tugged at his hair and screamed. "*Fourth caller*!" In complete despair, Barry dropped to his knees. "What does this mean? What does *any* of this mean?!"

He hunched over into the sand, tears streaming down his face. "Someone help me," he whimpered. "Anyone. *Please...*" A sobbing hiccup escaped from the young man, his eyesight blurring.

He needed a sign.

He needed a yes or no answer.

Was he right or was he wrong?

All of a sudden, Barry got his wish. The light, crackling sound of a campfire emerged in his ears. It was a pleasant sound, but not what he was looking for. Then the flames grew louder. Soon, there was a light shining above the blonde.

Barry rose his head up to look up in the sky. The moon, oddly enough, had been replaced with the sun. The night sky was gone, day had been born anew. And falling from the sky was what looked to be a comet or meteor.

"What the...?"

The ball of fire began to pick up speed, heading right towards the desert ground. The sight of such a doomsday element looked equal parts beautiful and haunting. A part of Barry wished it was the end of the world. His pain would end, and his divinity could allow him to start anew.

So, when the ball came barreling down for him, he simply closed his eyes and braced himself for the impact, his final sacrifice for the betterment of humanity.

...

Alas, no such sacrifice was made.

The ball of fire had crashed a few feet away from the blonde. The heat wafted through the air but didn't affect Barry much. The roaring crackling of the flames sounded like exploding dynamite. The impact upon the sandy floor of Death Valley was another explosive sound on its own.

Once Barry felt courageous enough to open his eyes, the heat waves blew into his eyes. He forced his eyelids down as the heat came and went. Once the inevitable cooldown arrived, the blonde opened his eyes and looked over to his left. The meteor had left a gaping crater in the ground, smoke flowing out of the hole.

The first thought that came to Barry's mind was a chimney, only the smoke was more spread out. It was obviously not the end of the world, and Barry didn't know whether to laugh or cry. The pain was to continue, the uncertainty hovering over his head like a black cloud. "Dammit," he muttered. "Dammit, dammit, dammit!"

The blonde slapped his hands into the sandy floor, hunching over. A nervous chuckle came out of him whilst tears dropped onto the sand. "*Fuck!*"

A moment of despair passed, and Barry soon felt courageous enough to walk over to the crash site. He stood up onto his feet and cautiously approached the smoke. The smell made the blonde cough and wave the fumes away from his face. The further into the smoke he trekked, the more his eyesight grew accustomed to the light hiding behind the cloud.

As he reached the edge of the crater, he knelt down so he could see the source of the crash. He waved the smoke out of his eyes again so he could get a better view. Alas, his efforts were in vain.

So, he inched closer.

And closer.

Until he had accidently gone too far and found himself falling into the crater.

"*Shit!*"

Barry rolled down the hole, crashing into the crater wall with hard thuds. Once he hit the bottom, he rolled until he hit something solid. With a groan, the blonde took a moment to gather his belongings. His limbs were horribly sore, and his joints ached like scrapes were forming on the flesh above them.

"Fuck me," he muttered to himself. With a deep breath, the blonde slowly pressed his elbows into the ground and pushed himself upwards. With another cough, Barry turned his head to the side. He opened his eyes and looked directly at the foreign object besides him.

It was a human body, skin charred from the flames. The corpse faced away from him, resting in eternal slumber on his side; or at least Barry assumed it was a man's body. The shoulders were certainly broad enough to be a masculine entity. The waist was also wide, lacking the curves of a more feminine form.

"Who are you?" Barry asked, not really expecting a response. Why he even bothered to asked was beyond his comprehension. Then again, everything about his experience in the desert was beyond his comprehension. For all he knew, the corpse might've turned his head and spewed Shakespeare for him!

When he was met with no response, he reached his hand over to the body's upper arm. Cautiously inching over, Barry closed his eyes and braced for the blistering hot touch. He grabbed onto the appendage; surprisingly cool. Re-opening his eyes, he turned the body over so he could see his face.

A cold chill ran up Barry's spine.

His fingers began to tremble.

The corpse hadn't completely burned, for there was still a fleshy face attached.

And he looked just like Barry.

"What the fuck?!" the blonde exclaimed. "What the actual *fuck*?!" And much more to the man's horror, the face blinked. "*Jesus*!" he gasped, quickly backing away from the body.

The charred corpse didn't move any further, aside from rolling his eyes to face the blonde. "Who are you?" the corpse asked.

Barry's eyes widened, mouth agape. "I-I-uh-I..."

The corpse blinked again. "I only asked a simple question."

The blonde swallowed an incoming breath. "B-Barry Waters."

Another blink from the body. "I see."

Barry's entire body trembled, his hands shaking. For the first time in days, he felt truly scared. Why did this effigy resemble him so? What was this supposed to mean?

"Who are you?" Barry asked, trying ease the fluttering in the pit of his stomach.

The corpse said nothing.

Not even another blink of acknowledgement.

Sick of the lack of answers, Barry glared at him.

"*I asked you a question*," he shouted. "I demand answers! Who are you? What's my purpose here? What's even going on?!"

The corpse didn't respond immediately, instead turning his head up so he was facing the bright sky. He stared, seemingly forlorn. "You serve no purpose," he said. "You're just food for the Sun."

Barry threw his hands up. "I don't believe that for a single fucking second! I've been suffering in his goddamn desert for days now! You can't tell me that it's all for nothing!"

The corpse slowly turned his head back to his side, giving the blonde a blank stare. "It's all for nothing."

Barry scoffed. "Absurd. Absolutely absurd. If I'm not a god, then why--"

Another blink from the charred body. "Are you going to keep making the same tired arguments? This is why you'll fall, too. Just like me."

Barry tilted his head to the side. "What do you mean? I'm down here, not up there. How can I possibly fall?"

"To lack such insight," the corpse commented. "Only means you'll fall faster."

The blonde shook his head. "I don't understand any of this. Stop being so cryptic!"

The body stared blankly at the college student. "Death doesn't discriminate, and neither does fate. You have hurt, now you will fall. It is the way of mankind."

Barry breathed heavily. "So...I'm not a god at all? What about the messages? My childhood?! Are you telling me they were all lies?!"

The corpse looked back up at the sky. "Your mortality is the only real truth. You'll do well to remember that in the next life."

And just like that, the corpse slumped over, dead. Tears continued to stream down Barry's face. Everything that he'd been led to believe for the last few days was a holy scam, a lie fabricated by the forces of nature.

All the horrible things he'd said.

All the horrible things he'd done.

They were all for nothing.

"What have I done?!" he wailed.

Chelsea's neck being stomped was a cruelty.

Rikki's body being used as body a flesh-light and meal was an even bigger cruelty.

But by far the worst cruelty of all was leading his friends to their final resting place.

"*Fuck*!"

Before Barry knew it, he was being kicked hard in the gut. With a yelp, he looked up to see Sasha. The brunette's eyes glowed with seething rage. "I found you."

The blonde sobbed. "Sasha," he pleaded. "Sasha, I'm so sorry. You were right about me. I'm a fucking monster. Nothing I can ever do will serve as an act of redemption for what I've done. Please, just--"

"*No*," Sasha barked. "You don't get to talk your way out of this."

Barry shook his head. "Sasha, please. I know the truth now. This guy beside me told me."

Sasha stared coldly at the blonde. "You're mad."

"No!" Barry sobbed. "I'm not mad! Just look next to me! You'll see..."

Surely enough, the corpse was gone. In fact, the entire crater had disappeared. He was lying on the flat sandy floor of the desert. Another horrible prank played by Death Valley.

"This is for Chelsea, you scumfuck."

Sasha lifted his foot up and began stomping as hard as he could into Barry's throat.

Chapter Twenty-One

Eyes Wide Open

Barry Waters looked up at the clocktower in the dead center of campus. It was his first day of college. He'd spent the entire previous day unloading his things into his dorm room. His room-mate was of little help, preferring to flirt with the nearby girls smoking in the courtyard. Even during the quick orientation seminar given later in the day, his roommate ditched to go score with a hot blonde girl from L.A.

But that mattered not, for Barry was mentally preparing him-self for his first period course, U.S. History. He'd left his dorm room thirty minutes early to give himself some time to navi-gate the campus. College was all about first impressions, and he wanted his to be a good one that spelled a punctual man, rather than one prone to tardiness. The size of the school was no excuse, in his opinion; the real world wouldn't wait around for him to find his way around a new place.

Thanks to his foresight, Barry managed to make it his class-room with only five minutes to spare. Luckily, most of his peers didn't seem to share the same logic behind being early to class. Only a small handful of students were seated at the elongated tables of the large classroom. On one end of the room were a gaggle of giggling girls all huddled up together. On the other end were a few scattered guys, laughing and cutting up.

And all by his lonesome was a handsome brunette, scribbling into a notebook.

Barry certainly didn't have the confidence to sit with the girls, and he didn't know the guys at all; he'd be an awkward third wheel! So, the choice was obvious to him; sit with the lonely brunette.

So, he made his way to the middle of the elongated table in the second to last row and plopped down next to the man. "Hey."

The brunette smirked. "Hey man."

"I hope you don't mind me sitting here," Barry commented. "I don't really know anyone here and I didn't want to sit alone."

The stranger shrugged. "Fair enough. All my friends went to different schools. So, I have room to make the acquaintance of another potential friend."

Barry chuckled. "Straight to business, huh? I can get behind that," he looked around the room, scanning to see if he could spot the professor. When he couldn't, he turned back to face his new friend. "I'm Barry, by the way."

The brunette looked back down at his notebook, continued to doodle on his college-ruled paper. "I'm Sasha."

The blonde chortled. "Sasha? Isn't that a girl's name?"

"Yeah," he confirmed. "If you're of American descent. My dad was born in Russia."

Barry nodded. "You don't sound Russian."

"Because I wasn't born there," Sasha explained. "I was born and raised in New York. My mom's from Buffalo. They moved to NYC before I was born, and the rest is history."

The blonde smiled. "Now I understand."

Sasha traced over a name on his notebook; one of which read "Chelsea". "What about you? Where are you from?"

"Eureka," Barry said with a quick nod. "It's up in north, near the very top of the state of California."

"Ah," Sasha acknowledged. "So, you're not far from home. I suppose that's a good thing."

"Yeah," Barry said, snooping on his new friend's doodling. "So, who's Chelsea? Girlfriend?"

The brunette smiled wide. "Yeah. We've been together for four years now. Started dating our freshman year of high school."

Barry whistled. "Damn! Four years is a long time."

Sasha chuckled. "Tell me about it. Her old man hated me for the longest time. He eventually warmed up to me, though. Never got to meet her mother, though. Never came around very often."

...

"Isn't that always the way," Barry remarked playfully. "Daddy's little girl can't be looked at by other guys or else they'll get a barrel to their face."

"You know," Sasha said. "Her brother actually welcomed me with open arms. First thing, too. We played football together in high school."

...

"Cool!" Barry commented. "You're lucky, I guess. Every girl I've ever liked would sic their brother or father on me. Never stood a chance, man."

Sasha smirked. "That's why you should be sneaky about it. Don't announce that you're going to bang the girl. Do it, then introduce yourself."

With a hearty laugh, Barry shook his head. "I don't know, man. My luck, I wouldn't even be able to snag a kiss, let alone a lay!"

"You lack confidence," Sasha said. "That's your first problem. Grow some hangers and make the first move."

Barry looked up at the ceiling. "You know, my dad also told me something similar. He said that won my mom over by being a nuisance," he chuckled. "The way he tells the story, he would hit on her every single day, and she'd always reject him. Eventually, she succumbed to his charms and said yes to a date with him."

"Now here you are," Sasha responded with a cheeky grin.

The blonde nodded. "Yeah," he looked back down at the door.

Still no sign of the professor; they were obviously running late. "I don't think I want to be that obnoxious, though."

"Maybe you'll find a girl that is low maintenance enough to not require such confidence," Sasha suggested. "I hear there's a pretty red head who is a freshman here, too."

Barry shrugged. "That doesn't narrow anything down. I've seen a couple of pretty red heads here."

"Yeah," Sasha explained further. "But this won the national dancing competition last year. And you know what they say about girls who can dance."

...

"That's very true," Barry commented. "You happen to know her name?"

"I don't know," Sasha said. "Rebecca? Rikki? Something like that. Her and Chelsea are roommates."

...

"Cool," Barry said with a grin. "I'm eager to meet her."

"You should be," Sasha remarked. "She's a fine piece of ass."

"I'm sure Chelsea wouldn't like hearing you say that."

The brunette shrugged. "I'm faithful and true, not blind and dead. I can look, so long as I don't touch."

"Understandable," Barry said. Being this far south from home

made the blonde think of the time he went to L.A. His father had wanted to see Metallica in concert for his birthday. Barry was just a young boy at the time, but he enjoyed the ride.

...

He'd even got to attend the concert with his parents.

...

The music was loud, but he soldiered through.

...

The trip was perfect.

...

And he often looked back wondering if he could ever relive such a magical trip ever again.

...

...

Chapter Twenty-Two

140 Degrees

Blood-soaked foot with a dead god beneath him, Sasha basked in the glow of his victory. Barry Waters was dead now. That not only meant he could ascend to godhood, but he could revive the innocent who had fallen. Rikki Simmons and Chelsea Franks were officially avenged.

Now they could arise from the dead with the use of Sasha's newly attained powers.

"I did it!" he screamed into the desert, his voice echoing. "I've slain the false god! Lay the divinity on me!"

He wasn't sure if it was the rising temperature or the birth of his godly abilities, but Sasha began to feel violently ill. It took much effort to keep himself from throwing up. The contents of his stomach, which solely consisted of bile at this point, rose up into his throat and he repeatedly swallowed to keep himself from losing control.

But this proved to be a feckless endeavor, for his soon puked all over the ground. The vile taste in his mouth ignited more sick to be released onto the sand. "Oh *God*," he groaned as he dropped to his knees. One more round of retching passed before he fell over onto his side.

His vision swirled and twirled like a ballerina, the pressure in his stomach and throat never ceasing. "No..." he moaned. "This...isn't supposed to be how this..."

Before Sasha knew it, he was seeing floating colors in his peripheral vision. They looked like little bubbles. If Sasha had the strength, he would've raised his hand to try popping them. Maybe they'd release some kind of serum that would be used to cure him of his current state.

Alas, his arms were dead weight. In fact, his whole body was dead weight. His bones had finally given out, his muscles and joints in constant agony. Either divinity was coming soon, or he'd been gypped. Was he any better than Barry at that point?

"I...I..."

Sasha couldn't finish his thought until a beautiful sight before him emerged. Walking toward him in the distance was a woman he thought he'd never see again. Her hips swayed, the Sun shining behind her. She looked like a million bucks, almost as if she'd never died.

"Ch...Chelsea."

It had worked, he thought to himself. He had revived the fallen. All it took was Barry's death to ensure the survival of everyone else. Now that the false god was gone, everyone could go back to their everyday lives.

The trip to Vegas would've never happened.

Sasha would've never met Barry Waters.

All would've been right in the world.

"I...am...your god."

Sasha's eyes closed permanently.

His body forever resting in the desert, providing a proper feeding for the buzzards.

Chapter Twenty-Three

Epilogue

The overall temperature in Eureka was cooler today than it had been for the last week. Then again, the morning air always brought a brisk chill to the northern parts of California. The chill was more noticeable in the suburbs than it was out in the city; there were simply more trees to breathe air into the atmosphere. And it wasn't so bad; it could've always been colder.

Kathleen Waters dressed in a way that allowed her to stay warm while also enjoying the chill. She wore a long sleeve shirt and khakis as she tended to her rose garden. Her husband, Gregory, lounged in his camping chair on the front porch. He wore shorts and a tank top, beer firmly grasped in his hand.

"Ah, to have a day off from the office," he happily mused before taking a sip of his drink. "It doesn't get any better than this."

Kathleen looked up from her garden and offered a smile grin. "Don't think you're going to laze around and not mow the lawn later."

Gregory playfully groaned. "Do I *have* to?"

"Yes, you do," she muttered, not buying into his attempts at frivolity. Her smile faded as she looked back down at her garden. Gregory caught on rather quickly that something was bothering his old lady.

"What's the matter? I know that low tone when I hear it."

The aging mother sighed. "I'm just...trying to get the house tidied up for Barry."

Gregory tilted his head to the side. "Why? Barry doesn't care how clean the house is. Have you *seen* his room?"

"He's bound to come home any day now," she argued.

The aging father blew air through his lips. "Kathy. Barry is living it up in Vegas right now. He's not going to visit for at least another week or so."

"Yeah," she snorted. "I'm afraid he's..." she held her fingers up to form quotation marks. "..."living it up" a little too much. He hasn't called in days."

"Relax, babe," Gregory instructed, taking another sip from his beer. "Barry's a grown man. And I have faith that we taught him well enough to not do anything stupid," he leaned further back into his chair. "Besides, we can't exactly boss him around anymore. He's moved out and in college. Let the kid have his fun."

Kathleen sighed and looked back down at her garden. "I

don't know, Greg. Something doesn't feel right. He never goes this long without at least a phone call."

Gregory smirked at his wife. "You worry too much. Barry is a Waters. No son of mine is going to be steered wrong in Las Vegas."

As she snipped a dead leaf off a rose, she breathed through her nose. "I hope you're right, dear." She stood up and admired her handiwork. Satisfied with the results, her rubbed her palms together before removing the gloves and dropping them onto the ground. As she'd obsessively done throughout the last couple of days, Kathleen pulled her cell phone from out of her back pocket.

She pressed the "home" button and the screen lit up. No missed calls, voicemails, or text messages. All that greeted her was a family picture from the time they all attended a Metallica concert. Barry looked so cute in his little Master of Puppets t-shirt. It had certainly been calmer, happier times.

"Where are you, Barry?" she asked aloud.

And suddenly, right on cue, two voicemail notifications emerged over her wallpaper. The aging mother's face lit up. "Can it be?" She clicked onto the first voicemail and held the phone up to her ear.

"*Hey Mom, it's Barry.*"

Kathleen smiled widely. "Greg! Barry called!"

"See?" her husband remarked before taking another sip of his alcoholic beverage. "I told you he'd come around."

Kathleen listened closely to the rest of the message.

"*Listen,*" Barry said. "*I need you to call me as soon as possible. It's an emergency. Love you. Bye.*"

The message ended and Kathleen wasted no time in calling him back. Much to her horror, she heard the worst possible message to hear when trying to call one's distressed child. "*The number you're trying to reach is unavailable. Please try again later.*"

The woman's hand immediately flew up to her mouth, her teeth baring down on her fingernails. "Barry's in trouble, Greg!"

"Barry's in trouble?" Gregory echoed, standing up from his chair. "What kind of trouble?"

Instead of responding to her husband, Kathleen pressed down onto the second message and held the phone up to her ear.

"*Mom,*" Barry greeted, desperation laced into his voice. "*Please call me. Please! We're stranded out in Death Valley. No water, no food, no air-conditioning, no car.*"

Kathleen nearly dropped the phone, her eyes widening. "My baby!"

Barry sobbed on the other end. "*Please Mom, I need your help.*"

Her heart broke into two. She hated hearing her child sound so downtrodden. Had she known this was going on, she would've jumped into the car and driven all the way to that damn desert; husband be damned.

But as much as she ached, her heartache was about worsen.

"Why aren't you answering me, you fucking bitch?"

Kathleen's jaw dropped. "Excuse me?!"

"Do you want me to die out here?"

"No, son!" she cried. "It's not even an option!"

"Well," he said, tone darkening. *"You better be lucky that you aren't here with me."*

Kathleen threw her hand up to her mouth, muffling her own cries.

"Because I will gut you like a fucking fish and feast on your intestines."

The aging mother screamed. What was going on? Why was he talking like this? Just how long had he been stranded out in the desert?

"You think I'm lying, you worthless cunt? Fucking try me."

The message ended and Kathleen was crying hysterically into her hand. "No!" she screamed.

Gregory watched her in horror. "Kathy," he asked as calmly as he could, given the circumstances. "What's going on? What did he say?"

She looked at him with frightened eyes. Before she could give him his answer, a car slowly pulled up to the driveway, flipping its blinkers. As the vehicle pulled in, Kathleen noticed it was a police cruiser. As the engine died, the police officer climbed out of the car. "Mister and Missus Waters?"

Gregory dropped his beer can, the aluminum bouncing off he pavement and alcohol spilling around his feet. Kathleens dropped to her knees, no longer bothering to cover her mouth. She screamed hysterically, loud enough for the entire neighborhood to hear.

Their ears didn't matter.

.

All that mattered was her heart.

An organ that would never be repaired.